Piers, Pliers and Problems

Sapphire Beach Cozy Mystery Series
(Book 3)

Angela K. Ryan

John Paul Publishing

TEWKSBURY, MASSACHUSETTS

Angela K. Ryan
John Paul Publishing
Post Office Box 283
Tewksbury, MA 01876

Publisher's Note: This is a work of fiction. Names, characters, places, and incidents are a product of the author's imagination. Locales and public names are sometimes used for atmospheric purposes. Any resemblance to actual people, living or dead, or to businesses, companies, events, institutions, or locales is completely coincidental.

Cover Design © 2019 MariahSinclair.com
Book Layout © 2017 BookDesignTemplates.com

Piers, Pliers and Problems/ Angela K. Ryan. -- 1st ed.
ISBN: 978-1-7340876-0-4

A Note of Thanks from the Author

I would like to warmly thank all those who generously shared their time and knowledge in the research of this book, especially:

Jacki Strategos, Premier Sotheby's
International Realty, Marco Island

Carol Buccieri
Bella Stella Beads, Haverhill, Massachusetts

Marco Island Fire Rescue
Marco Island, Florida

Any errors are my own.

Chapter 1

"THIS IS SO EXCITING," Grace said, as she arranged two dozen Italian cookies on a sky-blue serving dish. "How many students are registered for class tonight?"

"We have five members of the English Department from Florida Sands University: Jerry Morrison, a resident of Palm Paradise, who is making a necklace for his wife's anniversary present; Gertrude; and Emma," Connie Petretta said, as she set up a work station for each student and placed an array of tools on the large oak table in preparation for the evening's jewelry-making activities. "So, I will have eight students all together."

Palm Paradise was the condominium building overlooking the Gulf of Mexico, where both Grace and Connie lived. Connie had recently inherited the condo next door to Grace from her aunt and namesake, Concetta Belmonte, which lead her to relocate from the Boston area to Sapphire Beach, Florida, to open a jewelry shop. In addition to Connie's handmade creations, she also dedicated a significant portion of the store to selling Fair Trade jewelry, which inspired the name *Just Jewelry*.

"I'm proud of you, honey," Grace said. "That's a wonderful turnout for your first class. It should help to bring some traffic into the store during these slow summer months." The oppressive heat and humidity of southwest Florida tended to drive the snowbirds north and keep tourists away this time of year.

Connie agreed. "Plus, it will provide a way for me to share my love for the craft."

Grace's support meant the world to Connie. Not only had she had been Concetta's best friend, never leaving her side during her brief battle with cancer, but she was like family to Connie, as well. And her part-time help working in *Just Jewelry* was proving to be invaluable. Grace wasn't scheduled to work tonight, but she didn't want to leave Connie alone for such an important milestone.

Even in the midst of the oppressively hot summer months, business was better than Connie had anticipated. The grand opening in early April had been a huge success, and Connie saw a steady flow of traffic in the weeks that followed. Now that the slower months had arrived, there would be plenty of time to create jewelry and place orders with her Fair Trade suppliers in Kenya and Ecuador, so she would be fully stocked and ready to go by late September, when the snowbirds would begin to trickle back. So far, everything was going according to plan.

After preparing a place at the table for each student, Connie brewed two pitchers of iced tea, complete with fresh mint leaves from her plants on the patio behind the store, and placed the cookies that Grace had prepared on the table.

Most students would be attempting a necklace that Connie had chosen with inspiration from a fashion magazine. The only exception was eleven-year-old Emma who, with the encouragement of Elyse, Emma's mother and one of Connie's closest friends in Sapphire Beach, requested a simpler bracelet. Connie helped her choose a design that centered around a bead containing the letter E, for Emma.

Although *Just Jewelry* had only been open for three months, Connie was excited to add *teaching* to her ever-growing job description, which included *shop owner, Fair Trade vendor* , and *jewelry maker*.

Once everything was set up, Connie and Grace took a break on the overstuffed red sofa in the store's seating area, where they could see out onto the street through one of the floor-to-ceiling display windows. It was late June, and, because the brutally hot subtropical weather was in full force, there weren't many people walking around downtown Sapphire Beach.

Gertrude and Emma were the first to arrive, along with Elyse and Victoria. Victoria was a three-year-old little girl for whom Elyse and her police detective husband, Joshua Miller, recently began the adoption process, and Gertrude was Elyse's octogenarian great-aunt who was a delightful mixture of fun antics and wisdom.

Connie jumped up and hugged Elyse, Victoria, and two of her first students. She was beyond excited to begin this class.

"I'm so glad you and Victoria are staying to watch the class," Connie said, handing a chocolate chip cookie to the eager three-year-old. "It will be nice to have some friendly faces present."

"I wouldn't miss it for the world," Elyse said. "Besides, I want to be present as my daughter becomes a first-class jewelry maker," she said, winking at Emma.

"That's right," Gertrude said. "We could be witnessing history."

Within a few minutes, the rest of the students had arrived, beginning with the crew from Florida Sands University. They were led by a small, athletically built woman with dark brown hair that reached halfway down her back.

"I'm Isabel Spenser," she said, extending her hand to Connie. "This is Allister, Mary Ann, Paige, and Abby."

"Pleased to meet you," Connie said.

She recognized Abby's name as the person who registered the group. "We talked on the phone, didn't we?" Connie asked the young woman.

"Yes, that was me," Abby said, her gaze dropping toward the ground. She was a far cry from the enthusiastic young woman Connie had talked with the week before.

Isabel studied Abby for a moment, then continued with the introductions. "Allister here was just granted tenure. A few of us from the English Department decided to come out to celebrate his accomplishment. I'm Chair of the department, Mary Ann is my administrative assistant, and Paige is a graduate student, as well as Allister's teaching assistant. And, of course, you met Abby. She is our student worker and one of our most promising rising seniors."

Connie thought she saw Abby wince at Isabel's praise.

"Congratulations," Connie said to Allister. "What a wonderful way to celebrate your accomplishment."

"We thought we'd try something new to expand our horizons," Isabel said. "And maybe take advantage of the opportunity to do some team building as a department."

"Yes, some indoor team building under the air conditioning," Allister added, pulling his polo shirt away from his chest and fanning himself. "It's brutal out there. I'm not sure I'll ever get used to this heat."

Connie introduced the group to Emma and Gertrude and led everyone over to the table where they would be working. Grace poured them each an iced tea and offered them some cookies.

As they were settling in, the final student arrived.

"Everyone, this is Jerry," Connie said, gesturing toward a distinguished-looking man in his mid-fifties. "You know Gertrude," Connie said. Gertrude also lived in Palm Paradise. Then she introduced Emma and the folks from Florida Sands.

Jerry crossed his arms and studied Allister while Connie was doing the introductions.

A smirk making its way onto his mouth. "Not the same Professor Allister McCue who is teaching a summer poetry class on Wednesday evenings?" he asked.

"Yes," Allister said, puffing out his chest. "On the French Romantic Poets."

"My wife, Liz Morrison, is in that class," Jerry said with a sneer.

A look of recognition spread across Allister's face. "Oh, yes, Liz. She is quite lovely." He raised his eyebrows as he spoke.

"I agree wholeheartedly, Dr. McCue," he said in a possessive tone. "She left this morning for a business trip, so I'm taking advantage of the opportunity to make her a necklace for our twentieth anniversary next month."

Allister waved his hand. "Please, no Dr. McCue tonight." He made eye contact with Paige, then Abby. "From anyone. When we're not on campus, it's just Allister."

Connie watched Jerry, who was still closely observing Allister with a slight scowl on his face, and wondered what had gone on in Allister's class to warrant such contempt from his student's husband. Then she shook her head. She was better off not knowing.

Now seemed like a good time to begin class.

Chapter 2

SINCE IT WAS EVERYONE'S first time making jewelry, Connie began with the basics. She distributed the beads they would each need for their necklace, or bracelet in Emma's case, and gave each one a seashell-shaped mini-bowl to hold their beads while they worked. Then she demonstrated how to cut them free from their temporary wiring using a wire cutter.

When they registered for the class, Connie had given each student the option of using turquoise or orange beads for their necklace. Paige, Abby, and Isabel selected orange, while the other four chose turquoise. Since Emma's project was different, her beads were white.

Next, Connie introduced the tools that their first project would require, including two types of pliers, and helped them to cut the proper amount of bead-stringing wire. Finally, she provided the jump rings, toggle clasps, and other jewelry findings, which they would need to complete their necklaces.

While Connie taught, Grace refreshed the iced teas that were getting low.

"Congratulations on receiving tenure," Grace said, as she topped off Allister's glass.

He nodded his thanks while keeping most of his attention on his work. Once he got the wire through the tiny hole on the first few beads, he looked up at Grace. "Thank you. Sorry. I want this to be perfect. It will be a gift for a woman I'm seeing."

Allister's announcement brought silence to the room. Isabel's eyes remained glued on her work, but Mary Ann and Abby glanced up at Paige with what Connie interpreted to be an expression of concern.

Connie looked briefly at Grace, who discretely shrugged. There were clearly dynamics at play beneath the surface, but, whatever was going on, Connie was determined that the class would maintain a friendly tone.

Making her way around the table, Connie offered help to anyone who needed it. Gertrude turned out to be a quick study, and Emma, too, was absorbed in her work.

After a few minutes, Allister put down his work, apparently taking a breather, then leaned over to check out Paige's necklace. "You are so much farther along than I am. I think you have a knack for this," he said, looking at Connie for support.

"He's right," Connie said, admiring the beginnings of Paige's necklace. "You're good at this."

Jerry had looked up just in time to catch the interest that Allister had suddenly taken in Paige's work and shook his head in apparent disgust.

Allister ignored him, keeping his focus on Paige. "So, do you plan on working on your necklace all weekend, or do you have plans?"

She remained silent and didn't bother to look up until Abby kicked her under the table and shot her a glance that told her to be polite.

Paige put on a fake smile. "I have plans with some friends."

Mary Ann rolled her eyes at Isabel, who looked back down with a smirk.

Allister appeared to be nearly thirty years older than Paige, and she clearly wanted no part of him. Since Connie didn't want Paige to feel uncomfortable in her class, she pulled up a chair between the two and proceeded to distract Allister by giving him some pointers.

Appearing relieved that Connie had shifted Allister's attention away from her, Paige asked Abby if she was enjoying the book that she lent her.

"Oh, what book is that?" Allister asked.

Abby blushed. "Nothing you would approve of, Dr. McCue. I mean Allister."

"Oh, who cares whether he'd approve. We may be literature students, but that doesn't mean we can't enjoy some lighter romance books in our spare time," Paige said.

"Tell me you don't read the same garbage as Paige," Allister said to Abby. "You should feed your mind with the classics, even when you are pleasure-reading, so you can emulate those writers. Don't fill your head with useless trash."

Allister glanced at Isabel, but she either didn't see him or refused to make eye contact.

"I mean it," Allister said to Paige. "Only the best and brightest gain admission to our English Department. Don't waste your talent."

Connie glanced around the table while Allister was talking and thought she detected a flash of anger Mary Ann's eyes.

Isabel put her hand on Mary Ann's forearm. "Just ignore him. He didn't mean anything by that."

Mary Ann pulled her arm away and refocused all her attention on her the beads in front of her.

"Would you have any ice water?" Isabel asked Connie. "I spent the afternoon on my boat and am feeling a little dehydrated." Connie was happy for the diversion and wondered if Isabel changed the topic of conversation on purpose. Either way, Connie was grateful.

Elyse hopped up. "I'll get it. Victoria and I could use a little walk."

"I will never understand how you can afford a boat like the one you have on a professor's salary," Allister said. "Not to mention the condo in Cabo."

Connie half expected smoke to come out of Isabel's ears as she glared at Allister. "Not that it's any of your business, Allister, but I am fortunate to be a woman of private means." She managed to maintain a friendly tone, but her eyes were icy cold.

Allister smirked and turned his attention back to his work.

Elyse returned with fresh cups and two pitchers of water. Connie poured a cup for everyone, then left the pitchers in the middle of the table.

"Here you go, Isabel," she said, as she leaned past Jerry to give her the first cup. "Isabel is such a beautiful name. Does anyone ever call you Bella?" Connie asked, hoping to change the direction of the conversation.

Isabel seemed to transfer her agitation from Allister onto Connie. "No, I only go by Isabel. No Bella. No Izzy. Just Isabel."

Jerry leaned toward Connie, trying to suppress a smirk. "These creative types are so temperamental," he whispered.

She nodded in agreement and mouthed the words, "I know."

After offering pointers, answering questions, serving drinks, and repeatedly trying to steer the conversation to safer ground, Connie hadn't yet had a chance look at Emma's bracelet. She was pleasantly surprised at how well the girl was catching on. "Emma, you're doing a great job. I think you might have a future in jewelry making."

Emma beamed with pride and immediately got up to show her bracelet-in-progress to Elyse, but Victoria was squirming on her lap and Elyse had to stand. "It's beautiful, honey," she said, taking Victoria on a walk around the store.

Emma burst out in protest. "Can't you just stay here for a few more minutes? Victoria always needs *something*."

Gertrude tried to explain to her great-grandniece that three-year-olds needed a lot of attention, but Emma wasn't having it. She sulked and put her work aside. "I'm not in the mood for this anymore."

"I know how you feel," Connie said. "I have a little sister, too. They can be a real pain sometimes, but, in the end, I promise they're worth it." After a little more coaxing, she managed to get Emma to return to work.

Elyse smiled gratefully at Connie.

The one-hour class flew by, and before Connie knew it, it was time to wrap things up. She reminded her students that class would not meet the following week, since it would be the Fourth of July. The town of Sapphire Beach hosted annual fireworks that night, and it would be too chaotic to try to conduct a class. Besides, her students would likely have plans for the evening. The second and final session would be a week from Thursday.

Everyone took home their creations to work on them between now and the next class, and Connie encouraged them to stop by at any time to work on them in the shop or to ask questions.

After seeing Jerry and the Florida Sands group out, Connie leaned against the door and let out a sigh. "Well, that was an interesting group of people. There were clearly some underlying issues at play."

"I wouldn't worry about it," Elyse said. "You can't help it if they were a little strange. Maybe they'll warm up when they come back in a couple of weeks."

"Was Allister hitting on Paige, or was that just my imagination?" Grace asked.

"Yeah, that was strange," Connie said. "And if she's his student, it's probably against the school's policy, as well. I wonder why Isabel didn't say anything."

"Well, strange people aside, you did a fantastic job teaching," Gertrude said. "I learned so much tonight."

By the time everyone left it was after 8:00. Elyse promised to take Gertrude, Emma, and Victoria for an ice cream before dropping Gertrude off at Palm Paradise, and Grace decided to join them, so they left promptly.

Shortly after, Connie closed up shop for the night.

Chapter 3

CONNIE GOT UP EARLY on Friday morning to get in a quick workout before heading to the shop. She opted to avoid the oppressive heat and instead took the elevators up to the fourteenth floor, where the air-conditioned gym at Palm Paradise was located. After a stint on a couple of the cardio machines, she hit the heavy bag for a while. Not only did it allow her to work out her upper body, but it kept sharp some of those martial arts skills that she acquired, at her parents' insistence, when they learned she was going to volunteer in Africa after college. At the time she had taken self-defense classes to humor them, but it turned out she loved sparring, so she happily kept up the skill over the years. Plus, pounding the bag went a long way in working off any stress accumulating in her body.

After her workout, she took Ginger, the Cavalier King Charles Spaniel that she unofficially inherited from her aunt, for a walk, then headed back upstairs for a cold shower and some breakfast before making her way to *Just Jewelry*. With summer in full swing, Connie was expecting a slow day, so she planned to spend most of it making jewelry. Restocking her merchandise for the busy season was her top priority this time of year. From what she learned talking to other downtown shop owners, business would pick up in the fall, but January through April were by far the busiest months. Since she wasn't sure exactly what to expect for volume, her plan was to make as much jewelry as she possibly could and hope for the best. If she found her supply getting low towards Christmas, she could always place additional orders with her overseas artisans.

Grace normally worked on Friday mornings, but since she had helped with class last night, Connie insisted that she take the day off. Since Grace was her only employee, this meant Connie would be alone for the day.

After disengaging the security alarm, Connie filled Ginger's water bowl, then sat at the rectangular oak table to begin work.

Connie was excited to get started on this particular set. She fell in love with the sapphire blue pearl beads the second she found them online. She had also purchased slightly darker and smaller beads that would complement them beautifully. She would begin by making the earrings, since they would take the least amount of time, then move on to the necklace and bracelet. Since the necklace was an intricate pattern, Connie estimated that it would take about thirty hours to complete.

Connie reached for her favorite pliers among her jewelry-making tools, but they weren't where she thought she left them. *One of my students must have put them away in the wrong place last night*, she thought. She proceeded to open every drawer in the dentistry cabinet, where she stored many of her beads, then searched the storeroom out back. But still no luck.

She made a mental note to keep better track of her tools when there was a class going on. If she had to keep replacing them, the cost would quickly add up.

After grabbing another pair of pliers, Connie went back to the table to get to work. She hadn't noticed it before, but there was a woman's designer raincoat on one of the chairs. Connie knew the brand, and it was an expensive one. Whoever left it behind would certainly be looking for it. She didn't think it belonged to Grace, Elyse, or Gertrude, so if the owner didn't call by the end of the day, Connie would reach out to Abby to see if it belonged to anyone from the university. Since Abby had registered the entire group, hers was the only cell phone number Connie had.

Connie worked diligently, and about a half hour later, just as she was finishing the earrings, Elyse popped into the store with two iced coffees. "Hi Connie. I just finished a showing down the street, and I wanted to talk to you about something."

"Perfect timing," she said, eagerly accepting the coffee. "I was just about to take a break. I've been working on these earrings." Connie proudly held them up to show Elyse. "The necklace is going to take a while, but I thought I'd dive into some of the more intricate pieces now that I have the time and do

22

the less time-consuming ones as the store gets busier."

"Sapphire-colored beads for Sapphire Beach. That's perfect. I can't wait to see the finished products."

Connie led Elyse over to the couch. "So, what's so important that you wanted to tell me in person?"

Elyse rubbed the back of her neck. "I have some unfortunate news to share."

"Oh, no. Is everything okay with the kids?"

"Yes, it's nothing like that." Elyse seemed to be searching for the right words. "Josh got called back into work late last night, because there was a murder on the beach. Under the pier to be exact."

Connie gasped. "That's horrible. I'm so sorry to hear that. But why did you want to tell me in person? Was it someone I know?" Connie tried not to let her thoughts go wild. *Please don't let it be anyone I know.*

Elyse took a deep breath. "The victim was Allister McCue."

Connie felt her heart drop to the floor. "Allister was killed last night? After my class? There must be some mistake."

"It's no mistake. And that's not all. The murder weapon was a pair of pliers, like the kind you and your students were using last night."

Connie felt dizzy. This couldn't be happening. Her first jewelry-making class could *not* have ended in murder. It seemed so wrong that her pliers, a tool that she employed to make beautiful pieces of jewelry that brought people joy were used for something as ugly as murder.

"We'd better call Josh right away," Connie finally managed to say. "My favorite pliers, which we used last night, are missing. I looked everywhere but haven't been able to locate them." Given the circumstances, Connie had little doubt that the pliers in question were hers.

Elyse texted Josh, and within a half hour, he and Zach were at *Just Jewelry*. After seeing a picture of the murder weapon, Connie verified that it was indeed the same set of pliers that had disappeared from her shop. She had used them for many years and knew them well. She had no doubt they were hers.

"Who had access to these pliers last night?" Josh asked.

Connie pushed back the strands of dark hair that had fallen in front of her eyes while she studied the picture. "Literally everyone used them," she said. "Everybody's fingerprints, including Emma's, are likely on those pliers. We will be using the tools more in the next class, as students finish their necklaces, but I encouraged everyone to pass them around the table to get the feel of them."

"Can you remember who the last person was that you saw using them?" Josh asked.

Connie searched her mind, but she came up blank. "I remember Gertrude had them midway through class. Then she passed them along to Mary Ann. But that was well before class ended. They probably changed hands again several times after that."

"Did you see them after the class ended?" Zach asked. He had been so quiet up to that point that Connie almost forgot he was there. Since Josh was taking the lead on questioning her, Connie assumed that Sergeant Donahue had assigned Josh as lead investigator. But something seemed off about Zach. He was usually much more relaxed in her presence. Connie and Zach had gone on a date a couple of months ago, and he said he was going to call her to

25

take her out again, but she hadn't yet heard from him. Of course, he had gone home to Illinois for his uncle's funeral in May, then Josh and Elyse had taken a mini vacation earlier in June, so she knew Zach had been busy at work. But, still, his less-than-friendly demeanor told Connie that there was more to it.

Connie shook her head. "No. I straightened up a little after everyone left, but now that I think about it, I don't remember seeing the pliers after class. But I didn't put the all the tools away, because I knew I'd be making jewelry this morning, so it's possible they were still on the table. I mainly threw away the empty cups and washed out the pitchers of iced tea. Grace left right after class, so I know she didn't put them away. She doesn't usually touch my tools, anyway."

Josh jotted down some notes as they spoke.

"The only people with access to my pliers last night were those who were present at my class," Connie continued. A lump grew in her throat. "I can't believe that one of my first students is a killer." She looked at Elyse in horror. "And you were here with your girls." This was exactly the opposite of the atmosphere that Connie was working so hard to create in her store. She wanted *Just Jewelry* to feel like a home away from home for her students and customers, not the Wild West.

"I'm sure we weren't in any danger," Elyse said. "The killer obviously had a very specific target."

"She's right," Zach said. Why did he look like he'd rather be anywhere else? "We're going to need the names and contact information of everyone who was in the store last night during the class."

Connie booted up her laptop and jotted down the names, phone numbers, and emails that she had. Since Abby had registered the group from Florida Sands, aside from Gertrude's and Emma's, Connie only had contact information for Abby and Jerry. As she wrote the names of her first students, she felt more like a traitor than a successful teacher. This certainly couldn't be good for business.

"Aside from myself, Elyse, Victoria, Emma, and Grace, these are the people who were here last night," she said, ripping a sheet of paper with the requested information from a notebook and handing it to Josh.

Zach narrowed his eyes as if trying to remember something. "Didn't you get surveillance cameras after you were broken into a few months back?" he asked.

Connie nodded. "Yes. I'll email you the footage from the last twenty-four hours. It just shows the storefront and the back door, but you'll be able to tell if anyone broke in after hours and stole the pliers."

After the police left, Connie and Elyse went back to the couch and their half empty cups of iced coffee.

"Cheer up, Connie," Elyse said. "The police will get to the bottom of this. Besides, the murder happened on the beach. People won't even make the connection with your store."

But Connie wasn't comforted. "I was hoping these classes would become a popular activity in Sapphire Beach. You know, provide something different for people in the area to do. I was planning to offer an afternoon class for retired folks, and the evening classes could make a fun girls' night out. I had such high hopes. But who's going to want to come to a jewelry-making class that ends in murder? Plus, what am I going to do about *this* class? We're supposed to meet again in two weeks, but I doubt they'll come back."

Elyse put her hand on Connie's shoulder. "Take a deep breath. The police are going to catch the killer, and then they'll come back."

Connie put down her iced coffee and leaned back on the couch. "I hope so. I've worked so hard getting this business off the ground and spreading the word about my classes."

Elyse gave Connie a one-armed hug before getting up to leave. "Don't worry. You still have two weeks before the next class. A lot can happen in two weeks."

Chapter 4

AFTER ELYSE LEFT, Ginger hopped onto Connie's lap and rested her chin on Connie's shoulder, as if sensing her need to be comforted.

The dog's gesture brought a smile to Connie's face, and she leaned her cheek against Ginger's head. "What are we going to do, sweet girl? My first jewelry-making class ended in disaster."

For a moment, she wondered whether Allister would still be alive if she had scheduled the class for another day. Or if she had waited until the fall to hold her first class. Then she shook her head. There was no point in thinking that way. Connie couldn't have known that one of her students would be plotting evil while he or she sat around her table, a table where she had hoped friendships would be formed, not plans for murder. This *wasn't* her fault.

However, since Connie had been present during the last hours of Allister's life, perhaps a little investigating of her own was in order. After all, not only had the killer taken a life with Connie's pliers, but he or she had been plotting to kill Allister while she taught them how to make jewelry. The very thought of it made her blood boil.

Her first step would be to talk with the Florida Sands people to see if they could provide any insight. But it would have to wait until she could get some coverage in the shop.

Remembering that she had promised to email Josh and Zach the video file from her security cameras, she opened her laptop and created a file containing the past twenty-four hours of footage. Of course, she took the time to scan it herself before sending it over, but just as Connie suspected, it proved that nobody broke into her shop, using either the front or back door. It seemed unlikely that an intruder could have bypassed the alarm system and entered undetected, but the footage confirmed it. That meant somebody in her class took those pliers, most likely with the intention of killing Allister. Unfortunately, since the cameras only recorded the outside of the building, they didn't record the class, so she was unable to see who stole the pliers.

After she sent the email, Connie's stomach reminded her that it was past lunchtime. Since she was overdue to go grocery shopping, she hadn't packed any meals for the day. She glanced across the street to *Gallagher's Tropical Shack*. The lunch crowd had died down, so it would be a good time to grab a quick sandwich. She posted a sign on her front door that said, "Be back in five minutes," and made a beeline for *Gallagher's*.

Connie wandered into the bar area and took a table where she had a clear view of a window that looked out onto her store. If any customers came, she'd be able to run right over and reopen. Penelope, her friend and a server at *Gallagher's*, was waiting on a table in another station but came over to say a quick hello on her way to punch in an order.

Connie ordered a turkey club sandwich with sweet potato fries and answered a few emails from her phone while she waited for the food to arrive, looking up regularly to check on her store.

After only a few bites of her sandwich, her stomach felt like it was filled with rocks. For the first time since she launched her business, she felt pessimistic. Until now, every detail had painlessly fallen into place. She found Fair Trade vendors; her former boss, Sam O'Neil, was beyond supportive of her new venture; the shop renovations went smoothly; her grand opening was a success; and the first few weeks of business, before the snowbirds headed north, were fantastic.

She had been nervous about teaching a class for the first time and believed there would be a learning curve, but she didn't see *this* coming. Among her first students were a murder victim and, likely, a murderer. The more she thought about it, the more depressed she got.

She had to do something to shake herself out of this funk. Dwelling on the negative wouldn't serve any useful purpose.

Motioning to her server for a to-go container, Connie wrapped up her meal. Maybe her appetite would return later.

As she was signing the receipt, someone sat down in the seat across from her at her table.

She looked up to find Gallagher's friendly face.

He slid a plastic cup containing a green smoothie across the table. "If you're not going to eat solid food, at least drink this. On the house."

She gave him a grateful smile and sipped the smoothie. "Thanks, Gallagher."

"What happened to your appetite?"

"Did you hear about the murder on the beach last night?"

"Yes, some professor from the university was stabbed to death." He paused and smirked at Connie. "Wait, don't tell me you're connected to it somehow."

"Well, in a roundabout sort of way. Last night I had my first jewelry-making class…"

He interrupted her. "And the murder victim was your prize pupil?"

She reached across the table and playfully punched him in the shoulder. "He was one of my students. And likely, one of the others was the killer. Allister was stabbed to death with my favorite jewelry-making pliers."

"My gosh, Connie, you're like some kind of crime scene magnet. Maybe you should close up shop and join law enforcement."

"Very funny. Gallagher, what am I going to do? I can't run a store like this. Nobody is going to want to step through the doors."

"Are you going to do some investigating? I mean, I'm grateful for all you did to help solve Natasha's murder, but I'm guessing you couldn't stay away if you tried."

"I think I'll ask around a little and see what I can find out."

Gallagher shot her a playful smile. "You might want to start with the woman the victim was in here with last night."

"Allister was in here last night with a woman?" Connie asked. "Gallagher McKeon, you were holding out on me!"

"Nah, I would have fessed up. I just wanted to see how long it would take you to ask. He was in here with a young woman. She looked about half his age. Light brown hair. Ponytail. Khaki pants and a navy t-shirt."

"That was Paige. She's a graduate student in the English Department at Florida Sands University. They must have come in here after my class."

"She came in alone, but he followed shortly after and joined her over there." He pointed to a table right next to where they were sitting. "She didn't look thrilled to see him, but she reluctantly let him join her. When they finished eating, he insisted on picking up the tab. The conversation got heated, and I heard her say, 'Just leave me alone. I only want to keep our relationship professional.' I hung close by the table in case they caused a scene, but she got up and left and he followed right after her. When I saw his picture on the news this morning, I called the police and told them what I heard."

"Thanks, Gallagher." Connie said, "This gives me somewhere to start."

Connie returned to *Just Jewelry* and began work on the sapphire beaded necklace. Since Grace had the day off, Connie would be alone in the store all day, so she couldn't stop by the university to try to connect with Paige. Besides, Abby had registered everyone for the class and paid with a departmental credit card, so she really had no way of reaching

Paige or anyone else from the university. If only she could come up with an excuse to ask Paige to come by the store.

In any case, it occurred to her that she should call Abby and officially offer her condolences to the department. She looked up Abby's contact information. Fortunately, Abby had registered using her cell phone number in case Connie needed to reach her about anything outside of her limited office hours in the English Department.

She dialed the number, and Abby picked up right away.

"Abby, it's Connie from *Just Jewelry*."

"Oh, hi, Connie. I gather you heard about Dr. McCue."

"Yes, that's why I'm calling. I wanted to offer my condolences to you and the others. I am so sorry for your loss."

"Thank you."

"If there is anything I can do, please let me know."

"Thanks. We're still in shock over here. Isabel just hung up with Dr. McCue's sister who lives in California, which is where he is originally from.

She'll be flying in after the memorial service, which will take place in his hometown, to clear out his office."

"How is everyone holding up?"

"As well as can be expected. Mary Ann and I are okay, and Isabel has been crazy-busy all day. I honestly don't think it's hit her yet. She and the dean had to spring into action notifying students taking Dr. McCue's summer classes. She'll also have to find his replacement, which will be no easy feat. He was a prolific literary writer, in addition to a great professor. But I'm worried about Paige. She is really upset because of how cold she was to him in your class last night. She's really beating herself up over it."

Or perhaps she has a guilty conscience, Connie thought.

"I'm so sorry to hear that," Connie said. "Would it be possible for me to have her phone number? I would like to call her to personally express my sympathies. I will call Isabel and Mary Ann at their work numbers. I can get those off the university's website, but I don't have any way to reach Paige."

"I don't see a problem with that," Abby said. "She is a student in your class, so technically you should have everyone's contact info. Hold on. I have Paige's number programmed into my phone."

After a brief pause, Abby rattled off the digits.

Connie thanked her, offered her condolences once again, and hung up, pleased that she had Paige's number.

Connie immediately dialed the number Abby gave her, and Paige answered right away.

"Hi Paige, it's Connie from *Just Jewelry*. I heard about what happened last night and I wanted to offer my heartfelt sympathies. I just spoke with Abby, and she said you were taking Allister's death hard."

"Thank you, Connie. That is so kind."

"If you need to vent, feel free to stop by any time. I'm a good listener. And if you want to get your mind off things, feel free to take your necklace by the store. Business is slow this time of year, and I am just sitting here working on a necklace myself. I always find that keeping my hands busy helps keep my mind off my troubles."

"You know, I might just take you up on that. Dr. McCue's classes have obviously been canceled, so I have some extra time on my hands. As his teaching assistant, I would have been grading papers all weekend, but obviously that's no longer necessary. I'm going home to visit my mother tonight, but I'll try to come by tomorrow night."

"Come by any time. I'm here until 9:00."

After hanging up, Connie once again put up the "Be back in five minutes" sign and took Ginger for a quick walk. When traffic picked up in the fall, she would definitely have to hire additional help for Grace's days off. Then again, if word got out that her shop was a death trap, that might not be a problem.

Chapter 5

LATER THAT AFTERNOON, Grace came bounding into the shop, wearing a concerned expression on her face.

Her eyes darted around the store until she spotted Connie working at the table. "I just heard. I didn't have the TV on all day, but I ran into Gertrude in the lobby when I was checking my mail. Is it true? Was Allister McCue murdered last night?"

Connie stood and met Grace halfway across the floor, then guided her to a chair at the table. She wanted Grace to be seated when she broke the rest of the news to her. "Unfortunately, it is. And that's not all. The murder weapon was my favorite pair of pliers."

Grace put both hands on her head and stared back at Connie. Connie went to get them a couple of bottles of water while she gave Grace a moment to process the information. Then she rejoined her at the table.

"I feel like I need something a little stronger than water," Grace said.

"You and me both," Connie said with a chuckle. She filled Grace in on the conversations she had earlier with Gallagher, Abby and Paige.

A look of horror spread across Grace's face. "Wait, if Allister was killed with the pliers that were used last night, that means that one of your students stole the pliers to kill him."

"That seems like the most likely scenario." Connie narrowed her eyes. "The only other possibility I can think of is that the killer inadvertently took the pliers, and then killed him in the heat of the moment."

"Or perhaps, if someone took them by accident, the killer stole the pliers from one of your students," Grace suggested.

"No matter what happened," Connie said, "someone used *my* pliers to kill Allister. So much for a successful first class."

"Well, at least it will be memorable," Grace said. It looked like the shock was beginning to wear off.

Connie gave Grace a half-hearted smile. "True, but definitely not in the way I was hoping."

Just then, the front door chimed, and a happy diversion in the form of a customer entered the store. The woman headed straight to the Fair Trade section, and Connie told her in detail about the artisans, some of whom she knew personally, and the quality of their craftsmanship. The woman left with a smile and two bracelets, one for herself and one for her daughter. The interaction and the sale cheered Connie up and reminded her of why she had opened *Just Jewelry*.

After the customer left, Connie returned to the table, where Grace was still sitting and sipping her water. "I've been going over last night's class in my mind all day," Connie said. "There was definitely a lot going on beneath the surface, but did you observe any unusual behavior while I was teaching? Behavior that would suggest someone was planning a murder?"

"Let me think," Grace said, slowly rubbing her chin. "I don't know what people who are planning a murder typically look like, but Paige clearly wanted no part of Allister's advances. And Abby also seemed preoccupied."

"Yes, I agree. Abby was very enthusiastic, even bubbly, when she registered the group a couple of weeks ago. But last night she seemed to be a million miles away."

"Now that I think about it," Grace said, "there seemed to be tension of one kind or another between Allister and just about everyone there. I suppose certain workplaces can be like that, but even Jerry didn't seem pleased with him."

"That's a good point," Connie said. "He said his wife was in one of Allister's poetry classes and implied that he was flirting with her. Do you think that's a motive for murder?"

"I guess that depends on whether or not it went beyond flirting," Grace said. After a brief silence, she added, "All I know for sure is that we can rule out you, me, Elyse, Gertrude, and of course Emma."

Connie chuckled and nodded in agreement. "I guess that's a safe assumption. That leaves Jerry, Paige, Abby, Isabel, and Mary Ann. The question is, who hated Allister enough to kill him?"

Connie wished she could leave the store for a couple of hours and stop by the university, but it would have to wait until Monday. She didn't want to abuse Grace's generosity by asking her to work when she wasn't scheduled. But first thing Monday morning, she would stop by the English Department to offer her condolences in person and see who she could talk to.

A couple of more customers wandered into the store, to Connie's delight, and left with purchases.

When they left, Grace got up and gave Connie a hug. "I'd better go. I just wanted to make sure you were okay given everything that happened."

Connie flashed her a grateful smile. What would she do without Grace?

"I'll admit that I'm disappointed that my first jewelry-making class ended in a disaster, but it's not about me. I want the police to solve this horrible crime first and foremost for the sake of Allister's family and friends." Then she added, "But I'd be

47

lying if I didn't say that I'm concerned about the effect this could have on my business." Connie's gaze dropped to the floor for a moment, as she thought back on her first few months in Sapphire Beach. First, the previous shop owner disappears, then there is a murder after her first class, with Connie's pliers no less. And that doesn't even include what happened at Palm Paradise before she officially moved in. "People are going to start avoiding this place like the beach during red tide."

"You know what they say - any publicity is good publicity. Maybe you'll become a phenomenon, and people will line up all the way down the street."

"I'd rather be famous for other things," Connie said, "but thanks for trying to cheer me up."

After Grace left, Connie's cell phone pinged. It was a group text message from Elyse to Connie and Stephanie: *Is anyone up for meeting for drinks and appetizers tonight at* Surfside? *Josh is home so I am free any time after the girls go to bed.*

Count me in. How about 9:30? Connie replied.

A few minutes later, Stephanie replied. *I'm in. See you at 9:30 at* Surfside.

This was perfect. An evening with her friends was just what the doctor ordered.

***

Connie closed up shop at 9:00, drove the one-mile commute down Sapphire Beach Boulevard to take Ginger home, then left for *Surfside*. She arrived just on time.

Surfside was one of Connie's favorite restaurants in Sapphire Beach. A large deck with plenty of outdoor seating extended onto the sand, with the Gulf of Mexico a short distance away. The deck contained an outdoor bar, and several days a week there was live music, usually music that had been popular during the sixties and seventies.

Elyse and Stephanie had wisely secured a table under a fan and had already ordered some nachos.

Connie waved at Mandy, her favorite server and Elyse's former client, who was waiting tables in another section. Connie had to smile when she realized that she had only been there a few months, and between *Gallagher's* and *Surfside Resaurant*,

49

she already knew the waitstaff in two restaurants. She must be eating out a lot.

"It's such a hot night," Connie said, as she joined her friends. "I could go for a cold beer."

The others agreed, and they ordered three Coronas with lime.

Connie updated Stephanie on what had happened at her first jewelry-making class, then filled them both in on the conversations she had with Gallagher, Paige and Abby.

When their server came, Connie ordered coconut shrimp with rice pilaf and the other women ordered fried grouper sandwiches.

"Everything was going so smoothly with *Just Jewelry* up until now," Connie said, after the server left. "The grand opening was a huge success; business has been better than I expected during these hot summer months; and I was so excited that eight people signed up for my first jewelry-making class. But something like this could give me a bad reputation."

"Which means that you're going to take it upon yourself to investigate Allister's murder," Elyse said.

It was more of a statement than a question. Her friends were beginning to know her well.

The guilty expression on Connie's face gave her intentions away.

"Since there's no way we can stop you," Stephanie said with a smirk, "what are your thoughts on the case?"

"It's too soon to have any thoughts," Connie said. "All I know is that it had to be someone in my class who stole my pliers. Grace is working on Monday morning, so I'm going to stop by the university and see who I can talk to."

"Josh is the lead investigator on this one," Elyse said. "I know he and Zach are working hard on it. They're both worried about you, though. I think they've given up on trying to keep you out of their investigations, but Josh made me promise to tell you to be careful. Promise me you'll call one of them right away if you come across anything."

Touched by their concern, Connie promised that she would.

"Speaking of Zach," Stephanie said, "did you two ever go out on that second date?"

"No, not yet. In fact, I'm beginning to wonder if it's ever going to happen. Zach's been acting kind of strange lately."

"What do you mean?" Elyse asked.

"When he came into *Just Jewelry* yesterday, he was all business. It was as if we had no personal relationship at all."

"Wasn't he in there investigating a murder?" Stephanie asked. "He was probably just preoccupied with the details of the case."

"It's hard to explain what I mean. Even when he comes by for police business, he's not usually like that. Don't get me wrong, he's always been professional, but he's never been this... I don't know... distant, I guess. Something's up with him."

Elyse narrowed her eyes, as if in thought. "I wouldn't worry about it. He's probably just exhausted. Josh and Zach are the only detectives in the Sapphire Beach Police Department, and they have a big case load right now. They normally only work 9:00 to 5:00, Monday through Friday, but Josh has been called in on evenings and weekends several times this month, which means Zach probably has, too."

Connie popped the last coconut shrimp into her mouth and leaned back in her chair. "I really enjoyed our date, so I hope that's all there is to it. But I can't help but feel that something else is going on."

"I've seen the way he looks at you," Stephanie said. "I don't think you have anything to worry about."

"I agree," Elyse said. "I've known him for a couple of years, and I can tell he really likes you. If something is going on with him, it has nothing to do with his feelings for you. I'm sure he'll talk to you about it when he's ready."

Connie knew that they had had a great first date, but it was only one date. Who knows, maybe an old flame came back into the picture, or Zach could have decided he didn't want to date anyone right now for whatever reason. But Elyse was right about one thing: When Zach was ready, he would let her know what was going on. There was no point in dwelling on it.

"By the way," Elyse said, "we had a great time at the jewelry-making class. It's all Emma's been talking about. She even talks about it more than beach volleyball now, which is saying a lot. I think it might be her new obsession."

Connie laughed. "She certainly has a knack for it. Take her by anytime. I'm always game for helping an enthusiastic student. Who knows, maybe she'll have her own line of jewelry one day."

Elyse's expression grew pensive. "Thank you. I think I'll take you up on your offer. Emma could use a diversion these days. She's having a tough time adjusting to Victoria being in the family."

"I'm surprised to hear that," Stephanie said. "She seemed so excited to be a big sister at Connie's grand opening."

"She was. But I think the novelty wore off when she discovered how much time and attention a three-year-old requires. Emma's been an only child for eleven years."

"She'll get there," Connie said. "Just be patient with her."

When they finished dinner, the women prolonged the evening by taking a stroll on the beach. Before heading their separate ways, Connie invited them to *Just Jewelry* next Thursday evening, the Fourth of July.

"The annual fireworks display will take place from the pier at 9:30. I plan to have refreshments for customers, and I was hoping you would all stop by. When the store closes at 9:00, we can walk down to the beach and watch the fireworks together. I'll text you a reminder, and I'll include Zach and Grace in the message, but I wanted to tell you now so you could save the date."

They both agreed to come, and Elyse promised to extend the invitation to Gertrude, as well.

Chapter 6

ON SATURDAY MORNING, Connie set her phone alarm to go off a half hour early so she could swim some laps in the ocean before taking Ginger for her morning walk and getting ready for the day. Her new lifestyle in Sapphire Beach was proving to be much healthier than her previous one. She spent just as much time, if not more, working, but between walks with Ginger, all the outdoor activities at her fingertips, and having a gym right in her building, she was spending more time than ever before working out and filling her lungs with fresh air. Not to mention those regular doses of vitamin D from the Florida sun.

By the time Connie arrived in the shop, Grace had already swept the floor and was waiting on the first customer of the day. To Connie's delight, there was a consistent stream of customers, and the morning flew by. Just before lunchtime, Ruby, the owner of the souvenir shop next door, popped in for a visit.

"I wanted to talk to you about getting my store stocked with some Fair Trade handbags in the fall," she said, joining Connie and Grace in the seating area. "Is this a good time?"

The Fair Trade section in Connie's store had inspired Ruby to want to follow suit in her own shop. Connie was thrilled that she was setting a trend, and, depending on how things went for Ruby, she was considering pitching the idea to a few other shops in the area. If more stores carried items from Connie's Fair Trade vendors, it could have a ripple effect. Her contacts would be able to hire additional talented artisans in developing countries in need of employment, and she might even be able to expand to other countries and commission more vendors.

They talked about Ruby's needs and agreed on an order and pricing. Connie would place the order with her artisans via email and was confident that they would easily be able to fulfill it by October, when the snowbirds would begin returning to Florida after their summer up north.

Grace and Ruby had become fast friends, so when Connie and Ruby finished discussing business, the two women began chatting away. Ruby apologized for not being able to attend Connie's first jewelry-making class. "Even though this is the slow season, a lot of my employees are on vacation, and some are seasonal. So I haven't been able to break away from the store. Ironically, when it gets busy in the fall, I'll have more time. I promise to take a class then."

Connie shot Grace a questioning glance.

"You can tell her," Grace said. "Ruby is not a gossip."

Ruby looked curiously at Connie, waiting to be filled in, so Connie updated her on what took place after her first class.

As Ruby listened closely to everything Connie said, her mouth fell open. "Did you say this all happened on Thursday night?"

"Yes," Connie said. "Why do you ask? Did you notice anything unusual that night?"

"It might be nothing," Ruby said. "But I had a few tasks to finish up, so I didn't leave my store until close to 10:00 that night. When I was leaving, I heard a loud bang. I remember, because it made me jump. It turned out a man had angrily pounded his fist on the hood of his car. He was alone, but he was obviously angry about something. When he saw my scared expression, he apologized, but something didn't seem right about this man."

From Ruby's description of the man, Connie concluded that it was likely Jerry Morrison. She encouraged Ruby to tell the police what she saw.

"I'm so sorry your class ended this way, Connie, but I hope you realize it's not your fault," Ruby said. "Someone obviously stole your pliers, so whatever problem the killer had with Allister, he or she brought it with them to your class."

"I know," Connie said. "It's just not how I wanted my teaching debut to go."

"Don't worry. The police will get to the bottom of everything, and, before long, it will be yesterday's news. Perseverance is the name of the game, and I can tell you're a tough cookie. You'll make it through this. I'll help spread the word as soon as you set a date for the next class."

"Thank you," Connie said, squeezing Ruby's forearm. "It helps to know you're in my corner."

By the time Ruby left, Connie was feeling better about the situation. Something about Ruby always lifted Connie's spirits. She had a way of talking that made you believe she'd lived through the exact same thing and came through it victoriously. Connie couldn't help but wonder about her life and hoped that one day soon she would learn more.

Saturday afternoon dragged on as Connie struggled to keep her mind off Allister's murder and on more productive things, such as updating her social media pages and website with new photos. She was looking forward to talking with Paige later that evening and hoped that she would still come by the store as she said she would.

Connie had to force Grace to leave about mid-afternoon, because she was spending too much time at the store. It wasn't that Connie didn't want to pay her for additional hours; she just didn't want Grace to burn out in the first few months of business. Connie wanted Grace to be with *Just Jewelry* for a long time. There was no doubt about it - she would definitely have to hire additional help before too long.

At 7:00, Paige came by to work on her necklace, as promised. The two women settled into their workstations at the oak table, and Connie helped Paige to pick up where she left off Thursday night.

After a few minutes, it became obvious that Paige's heart wasn't in it. She kept glancing over at the chair that Allister had occupied the night before, and she finally voiced what she was obviously thinking. "I can't believe Allister was sitting there just the other night. Who could have imagined what would have happened?" Then her face became distorted with pain. "I was so abrupt with him. I wouldn't even give him a straight answer when he asked about my weekend plans."

Paige was either a good actress or truly distraught about his death. Or maybe the pain on her face was guilt.

Connie gave her the benefit of the doubt and tried to comfort her. "Well, your plans *are* your own, and he had no right to ask."

"I know," she said, appearing to recover herself. "I go back and forth between being enraged that he put me in that position and guilt for not being kinder."

Connie thought about her conversation with Gallagher. "Paige, is it okay if I ask you a question about Allister?"

Paige shrugged. "I guess."

"I had lunch over at *Gallagher's Tropical Shack* yesterday afternoon. I heard you and Allister ate there together after class and that the two of you got into a heated argument."

She looked down and nodded. "Yeah, that's true. He just wouldn't let up. He kept trying to get into my good graces, but I knew he was a player, and I didn't trust him. I feel terrible that he's dead, but there was no way I wanted him anywhere near my mother."

Come again? "Your mother?" Now Connie was confused. She thought Allister had been hitting on Paige.

"Yes. About a month ago my mom stopped by the English Department to pick me up, because we were going to lunch. She recently retired to this area, which was part of the reason I chose Florida Sands for grad school. I was tied up with something, and Allister didn't hesitate for a minute to move right in. Before I knew it, he had a date with her, and they've gone out every weekend this month. He'd been trying to get in my good graces ever since."

Connie leaned back in her chair. That explained why, when Allister said he was making his necklace for a woman he was dating, everyone grew silent and watched Paige's response. Connie had falsely assumed that Allister had been hitting on Paige and that he was hoping to give *her* the necklace. She was glad she hadn't voiced what she was thinking. That could have been awkward. "And since Allister was your professor and boss," Connie clarified, "you just wanted him to stay out of your personal life."

"Exactly. As his TA, he was my superior and he was even my advisor for my doctoral dissertation. How was I supposed to know if he really liked my work, or if he was just kissing up to me because he was dating my mother? But more importantly, I didn't trust the guy with my mom."

"Don't be so hard on yourself, Paige. You had a right to your feelings. It did put you in an uncomfortable situation."

"You don't think I'm a monster for the way I treated him?" Paige asked.

"Not at all." Connie thought about how she would have reacted in a similar situation. What if her parents were no longer married and a guy who Connie knew to be a player was after her mother? Not to mention the power differential that was at play. Talk about a no-win situation. "I think I would have done the same thing if I were in your shoes," Connie said.

Although it could still be a motive for murder, Paige was looking less like the killer. If she felt that badly about being unkind to Allister, she probably wouldn't have been capable of murdering him. And with pliers.

But then again, according to Gallagher, she was pretty angry at Allister when they left the restaurant on Thursday night, and, as far as Connie knew, she was the last person to see him alive. It's possible she's hiding something about herself, but it wouldn't hurt to see what she knew about the others.

"Paige, do you have any idea who might have killed Allister?" Connie asked. "I don't mean to scare you, but the killer was most likely in my class on Thursday night. Did anyone in the English Department have a grudge against him?"

Paige looked down, as if contemplating whether she should share something.

"What is it? Please tell me if you know anything that could lead to Allister's killer. I want my students and my customers to feel safe in my store."

"It's probably nothing, but Abby was in one of Allister's English classes – one where I was his teacher's assistant."

"Go on," Connie said.

"Well, nobody knows this, because Allister didn't have a chance to report it yet, but he caught her plagiarizing on one of her papers. He was going to turn her in to the Dean of Students. Abby insisted it was an honest mistake, but according to the university rules, it doesn't matter. The penalty is quite stiff, and she would likely have been expelled. At a minimum, she would fail the course and be put on academic probation."

"Isn't Abby a promising student?" Connie asked.

"Yes, she's in the top of her class. In September, she will begin her senior year, and with her talent and grades, she could get into any graduate program she wants. And that's her plan. To become a professor and a writer. That kind of blemish on her record could ruin everything."

Both Connie and Grace had noticed that Abby was preoccupied the night of class. This must have been what was on her mind.

"Do you think she's capable of murder?" Connie asked.

"I wouldn't have thought so, but it's hard to tell. She is very driven, and she's wanted to be a professor and a writer since she was a kid. Who knows what someone is capable of doing to protect their lifelong dream?"

Connie couldn't argue with that.

"Since you're investigating, there's one more thing you should know," Paige said. "Allister and I weren't the only ones from your class in *Gallagher's* on Thursday night. Jerry had been sitting at the bar the whole time while we ate. He just nursed his beer and stared straight ahead. He had this pained expression on his face, as if something was eating away at him. As we left, he was walking behind us and when I drove away, neither Jerry nor Allister had gotten in their car yet."

That was interesting. It most likely *was* Jerry who scared Ruby by angrily banging on his car Thursday night.

Chapter 7

AFTER PAIGE MADE a few more unsuccessful attempts to concentrate on her necklace, Connie could see that she was ready to call it a night.

But before Paige left, there was one more thing that Connie wanted know. She had been struck by how angry Mary Ann suddenly became with Allister on Thursday night when he talked about only the best and brightest being admitted into Florida Sands. Connie remembered the anger that filled her eyes and Isabel's comment that Allister didn't mean anything by it, so she asked Paige what that was all about.

"I noticed that, too," Paige said. "I think it's because Mary Ann's son, Ian, was denied admission to Florida Sands. She must have taken Allister's comment as a jab. That probably wasn't the way he meant it, but she's really sensitive about it."

As Paige was leaving, Connie encouraged her to return any time to pick up where she left off. She wanted her students to feel as though *Just Jewelry* was their home away from home. Even though Allister's murder meant that things were off to a less than perfect start in that department, she was still determined to do everything in her power to provide a welcoming atmosphere.

After tidying up, Connie closed up and went straight home, where she spent the rest of the evening relaxing on her balcony, with Ginger at her feet, breathing in the salty air. A consistent, gentle breeze blew off the Gulf, making the heat and humidity bearable.

On Sunday morning, Connie attended the 7:00 Mass at Our Lady, Star of the Sea parish, then headed into the shop early. The sun was strong in the sky, and it was already hot. The weather app on her phone informed her that it was eighty degrees and climbing, with sixty-five percent humidity. She laughed when she read, "Feels like ninety-nine degrees." *That sounds about right.*

The Cavalier King Charles Spaniel calendar that Grace hung behind the checkout area reminded Connie that it was the last day of June, which meant the Fourth of July was right around the corner, and she hadn't sent that text yet inviting her friends to her shop.

She sent a group text to Elyse, Josh, Zach, Grace, and Stephanie, and, at the last minute, she added Gallagher and Penelope. She didn't expect that they would be able to come, since the restaurant would likely be busy until late that night, but she wanted them to know they were invited. Of course, Josh or Zach could be called in to work at any time, but she hoped that wouldn't be the case.

Connie thought about Zach's behavior the last time she saw him. She would give him another week, and if he didn't reach out, she decided she would ask him about it. Whatever was going on with him, Connie was determined not to let his behavior get her down. If he was no longer interested, that was his prerogative. His sudden coolness just seemed so uncharacteristic. She said a prayer that everything would work out for the best. Whatever *the best* was.

By the end of the day, she had heard back from everyone, except Zach. When Elyse called to see what she could bring, Connie mentioned that Zach hadn't responded yet. Elyse assured her that she would have Josh check in with him, since they were meeting up for dinner with some friends.

Later that night, as Connie arrived home, Elyse called.

"You're right. Something is definitely up with Zach. After dinner, Josh got him alone and tried to talk to him. Zach told Josh that there *was* something going on with him, but he couldn't talk about it. He insisted that he just needed some space to sort through some things."

Connie's heart sank. Her first thought was that she hoped he wasn't having any health issues. She thought back to when she saw him on Friday morning, and he looked healthy. Nevertheless, she said a quick prayer that he was okay.

"I thought Zach and I were friends," Connie said. "What could be going on that he wouldn't talk to me? He must no longer be interested."

"I don't think that's the case," Elyse said. "Just give him some time. He'll talk to you when he's ready. Besides, he did say he's coming on Thursday night. He and Josh will both be there unless they get called into work. He's going to text you to confirm."

Sure enough, Connie received a text from Zach later that night. *I'll be there on Thursday. Looking forward to it.*

***

On Monday morning, Connie texted Grace to inform her that she had to make a stop before work and would be arriving at the store a little late. Then she headed north on Route 75, and, after stopping for flowers, arrived onto the campus of Florida Sands University.

With the help of an online map, she easily found Alumni Hall, the white stucco building that housed the English Department. She parked in a nearby parking lot and headed toward the building.

Outside the front entrance, she spotted Abby sitting on a blanket under the shade of a majestic mahogany tree, absorbed in a book.

"Hi Abby," Connie said, trying not to startle her.

But it was too late. Abby inhaled sharply and jerked her head toward Connie, putting her hand on her chest.

"Sorry," Connie said. "I didn't mean to sneak up on you."

Abby smiled. "No worries. I guess I'm a little on edge these days. I thought it would be nice to get some fresh air, but it feels like an oven out here. Even under the shade."

"Do you mind if I sit down for a minute?" Connie asked.

Abby scooted over on the blanket and Connie sat down, placing the flowers she had brought on the grass next to her.

"I thought I'd stop by and offer my condolences to the rest of the English Department," Connie said. "I spoke with Paige on Saturday, but I still haven't had a chance to talk with the others."

"Everyone is walking around the department looking shellshocked," Abby said. "I only work a few hours a week in the summer and wasn't scheduled to work yesterday, but I volunteered my time to help out by answering the phones. I figured I could at least take one task off their hands."

"I'm sure they appreciated your help," Connie said.

A frisbee glided in their direction and landed on the grass a few yards away, so Connie jumped up and sent it flying back to one of the students playing in a grassy area, just beyond the building. The scene made Connie miss college life.

"How are your studies going? I understand you are in the top of your class."

Abby looked as though Connie had punched her in the gut, not the reaction to her compliment that Connie expected.

"Yes," Abby said. Her tone was more solemn than enthusiastic. "I am planning to get my doctorate and hopefully teach one day. It's been my dream forever."

Connie thought of her own windy journey that took her to where she was today. "It's pretty unusual to know exactly what you want in life from such a young age."

Abby pulled her knees to her chest and gazed into the distance toward the two students tossing a frisbee. "Books got me through some really tough times as a teenager," she said. "I got diagnosed with leukemia when I was fifteen years old. In January, I celebrated five years in remission, and the doctors are optimistic. When things were at their worst, I decided then that if I recovered, I would spend my life writing and sharing with others my love for literature. That dream helped me pull through, and I've never wavered from it."

"Wow, that's a beautiful story," Connie said. "And are you still on track to accomplish your goal?"

Abby gave Connie a confused look, so Connie decided on the direct approach.

"Abby, I have to ask you a tough question." She paused for a moment, then continued. "Was Allister going to turn you in to the Dean of Students for plagiarism?"

Abby's eyes shot wide open and she appeared to scan her mind, trying to understand where Connie got this information. "Did Paige tell you that?"

The last thing Connie wanted to do was get Paige in trouble.

"She mentioned it, but don't be mad at her. She came by *Just Jewelry* on Saturday to work on her necklace, and I asked her about each person she knew in the jewelry-making class and what they might have against Allister. For the record, she doesn't think you would have hurt him. We were just thinking aloud."

Connie hoped that would smooth things over.

Abby looked down and tightened her shoulders. "She's right. I was angry that Dr. McCue was going to report me. I thought he should at least give me a second chance, given that it was an honest mistake. But I never would have hurt him."

Connie sincerely hoped Abby was telling the truth. "Do you have any idea who else might have benefited from Allister's death?"

Abby stroked the spine of the paperback book that she was still holding. "I've been thinking about that since I found out he was murdered. It had to be someone from the jewelry-making class, since we were the last ones with access to the pliers." She put the book down on the blanket and glanced around before continuing. "Dr. McCue was respected here, but not necessarily well-liked. Both Dr. Spenser and Mary Ann had their problems with him, and neither wanted him to receive tenure." Abby paused. "But I *will* say that the last person I remember seeing with the pliers was Mary Ann."

Connie leaned back on her palms. "People don't usually kill because they don't like a person. There would have to be a stronger motive than that."

"I know for a fact that Dr. Spenser recommended that Dr. McCue be denied tenure. I think she was jealous of the fact that he consistently got more articles published than she did. She may have even been afraid that he would go after her job at some point. As for Mary Ann, I don't know why she hated him so much, but I know she did. It was obvious to everyone. When Mary Ann learned that Allister got tenure, she was visibly upset. I think she was hoping he would be denied and be forced to relocate. They rubbed each other the wrong way."

"Why wouldn't she just quit?" Connie asked.

"Probably because she likes working for Dr. Spenser. She's good to her employees and gives Mary Ann a lot of freedom. She even lets her leave work to pick up her daughter from school every day. Mary Ann's job was perfect except for Dr. McCue. Plus, he would openly make fun of her for reading what he called 'trashy novels.'"

"Trashy novels?"

"Yeah, he was kind of a literary snob. He called anything he didn't approve of 'trashy', including some good books. Even Isabel would roll her eyes when he would go off on one of his haughty tangents."

Chapter 8

CONNIE WAS EAGER to get out of the heat and into the air conditioning, so she excused herself and climbed the cement stairs leading into Alumni Hall, the building that housed the English Department.

She followed the signs up to the third floor and found Mary Ann seated at the front desk talking with Isabel. Mary Ann stood to greet Connie, who handed her the flowers she had brought.

"I'm sorry to interrupt your morning. I know this is a difficult time for you, but I wanted to stop by and offer my condolences in person."

"Thank you, Connie," Isabel said. "That's very kind of you."

"I keep expecting Allister to walk through the door," Mary Ann said. "It's all so surreal."

Isabel nodded solemnly. "I appreciate your coming by, Connie, but I must excuse myself. Summers are usually quiet around here, but with everything that has happened, I have a long list of tasks to accomplish today."

"Of course," Connie said.

Isabel disappeared into her office, leaving Connie alone with Mary Ann.

"The police have been in and out of here several times in the past few days. They told us that the murder weapon was a pair of pliers from the jewelry-making class," Mary Ann said.

"Yes, that's true. I confirmed it with the police on Friday morning. They disappeared from my shop some time during class."

Mary Ann shook her head and let out a deep breath. "That means the killer was with us in class."

"It appears that way. I sent the police surveillance footage from my security cameras on Friday morning. They only capture the exterior of the store, but maybe they'll be able to find something."

Connie studied Mary Ann as she moved busily about the office. She pulled a vase from the cabinet behind her desk, filled it with water from a nearby water cooler, and placed it on a coffee table in the reception area. When Connie finally had Mary Ann's full attention, she asked, "Do you know who could have done this to Allister? Did he have any enemies within the department?"

Mary Ann looked skeptically at Connie. "I'm sure the police will conduct a thorough investigation. Why don't we just leave it to them to ask the questions?"

"I'm sure they will," Connie said. "But I kind of take it personally when somebody steals my pliers to kill one of my students. I think I have a right to ask a few questions."

Mary Ann relented. "Fair enough. Allister certainly could be... shall we say, challenging, to work with. And academia is known for being competitive. But I can't imagine anyone hating him enough to kill him. Of course, Allister and I had a wonderful working relationship," she added. "I was thrilled when he got tenure."

Either Abby had been trying to throw Connie off, or Mary Ann was lying through her teeth about her esteem for Allister.

A reflective expression came across Mary Ann's face.

"What is it?" Connie asked.

"Oh, I was thinking about Jerry, from class. He was not a fan of Allister. One evening a couple of weeks ago, as I was leaving, Jerry was dropping off his wife for class. Allister had just pulled into the parking lot. Jerry got out of the car to open the door for his wife, and it was like there was smoke coming out his ears at the sight of Allister. When Allister and Liz walked to class together, Jerry started asking me questions about Allister and insinuating that he was a playboy after his wife."

"Was there any truth to that?"

Mary Ann shrugged. "I doubt it. Allister *was* kind of a player. But I don't think he was involved with Jerry's wife."

"But if Jerry believed he was…" Connie said.

"Exactly. I was shocked to see him at your class. I'm not sure if you picked up on it, but you could have cut the tension with a knife when Jerry walked in. And Paige being there only added to the tension. She used to get furious when Allister would hit on women in front of her, but you can't blame her, considering his relationship with her mother."

Connie nodded to show that she was aware of the situation.

While they were talking, Mary Ann's desk phone rang. "I'd better get back to work. The phone has been ringing off the hook, and with everything that's happened, we're so behind."

"Of course. If there's anything I can do, please let me know."

Mary Ann gave her a thumbs up as she answered the call.

On her way out, Connie peeked her head into Isabel's office. "Isabel, I just wanted to say again how sorry I am for your loss. If there's anything I can do, please don't hesitate to contact me. And if you want to get away from here for a little while, please feel free to come by the shop to work on your necklace."

Isabel briefly looked up from her computer. "Oh, I doubt I'll be able to work on the necklace anytime soon, but I do appreciate the thought. But, Connie, I was going to call you to see if I left my rain jacket in your shop. I can't seem to find it, and I'm pretty sure I had it with me on Thursday evening."

With everything that happened, Connie completely forgot about the jacket. "Yes, I did find a raincoat over one of the chairs on Friday morning. I'll bring it by tomorrow morning before I head to the store."

"Don't bother. I have another. I'll stop by to pick it up next time I'm in the neighborhood."

"Okay, but it's no trouble." Connie handed Isabel a business card. "If you change your mind, just call the shop."

On her way to work, Connie stopped by Palm Paradise to pick up Ginger. She hadn't meant to leave Grace alone in the store for so long, but it turned out not to be a problem. It had been quiet so far, with just a couple of customers who were only interested in browsing.

Connie took advantage of the slow morning to work on her necklace, while Grace waited on the occasional customer who wandered through the door. Around lunchtime, Grace volunteered to pick up sandwiches so Connie could continue to work.

As they ate, Connie filled Grace in on her morning at Florida Sands.

"It sounds like just about everyone had a motive to kill Allister," Grace said.

Connie leaned on the table and let out a deep sigh. "I was thinking the same thing. I'm no closer to receiving any answers than I was on Friday morning."

After throwing away their empty sandwich wrappers, Connie wiped down the table. "Thanks for lunch, Grace. What are your plans for this afternoon?"

"I was thinking, Connie."

"Uh oh," she teased.

Grace waved her hand dismissively at Connie. "I'm serious. You haven't had much time off since you opened *Just Jewelry*. Why don't you take the rest of today off and do something to get your mind off Allister and the store. I think you need a mental health day."

Connie laughed. The offer was tempting, but she didn't want to wear Grace out.

Connie thought for a moment. "I'll make a deal with you. I'll take the rest of the day off if you agree to take Wednesday off. I appreciate what you're doing, but we both need to make sure we don't burn ourselves out."

"Okay then, it's settled. Get out of here," Grace said, leading Connie to the door.

When Connie and Ginger returned to Palm Paradise, they headed straight for the beach. Once the dog realized where they were going, she pulled Connie with all her might across the silky white sand towards the waves, gently crashing on the shore. As Ginger enthusiastically chased away the sandpipers and seagulls waddling along the hard sand, she also managed to chase away Connie's anxieties over all that had been happening. The diversion was well worth the extra bath that Connie would surely have to give Ginger afterwards.

While Connie and Ginger splashed around by the water, her conversations about Jerry with Paige and Mary Ann kept swirling around in her mind. Jerry's dislike of Allister had been clear during class, but how deep did his feelings run? Mary Ann's story seemed to confirm that Jerry believed Allister was after his wife. But why did Jerry follow Allister and Paige out of *Gallagher's*, and what happened between Allister and Jerry after Paige left? Ruby heard Jerry pound his fist on the hood of his car, so he was clearly angry. Was he angry enough to follow Allister to the pier and kill him?

Connie was anxious for answers. Before leaving the beach, she determined that she would pay Jerry a visit this evening. Since they both lived in Palm Paradise, it should be easy enough to think up an excuse to stop by and see what she could learn.

On her way back up to her condo, Connie checked the mail and found Gertrude seated in an armchair and holding court with some residents. They were discussing Allister's murder.

Gertrude extended an arm to Connie as she walked by with her mail. "Connie, come here sweetie. How are you doing? You must be devastated about what happened on Thursday night."

Connie gave her a light one-armed hug and flashed the other women the friendliest smile she could manage. She didn't want to show her full level of concern in front of the others, so as not to scare them off from her shop. Fortunately, it appeared as though Gertrude hadn't brought up the fact that Allister was killed with her pliers.

Connie broke free as quickly as she could politely manage, and brought Ginger upstairs, narrowly avoiding getting embroiled in neighborhood gossip.

With the help of some sweet-scented doggie shampoo, Ginger was smelling like her old self in no time. Connie gave her a rawhide bone as a reward for being good during her bath, then booted up her laptop and opened Jerry's class registration form, where his address was listed. He and Liz lived in Unit 1010. Perfect. She felt a passing twinge of guilt since she was supposed to be using her afternoon off to clear her mind of anything related to *Just Jewelry* and Allister's murder, but what Grace didn't know wouldn't hurt her.

Connie put some chicken and potatoes in the oven to bake and tossed a small salad. When the chicken and potatoes were cooked, she turned off the oven and left them inside to stay warm while she paid Jerry a visit. She took the elevator up three floors, and within a few minutes, she was standing in front of Unit 1010. Jerry must have been on his way out, because he immediately opened the door with his car keys in hand. He stared at Connie as if in a daze.

"Jerry," she said, "I'm sorry to stop by unannounced. I just wanted to check in and see how you were doing after everything that happened Thursday night. I'm sure you heard about Allister McCue."

An attractive woman with a dark bob, who Connie assumed to be his wife, Liz, appeared behind Jerry, and it suddenly occurred to Connie that Liz wasn't supposed to know about his jewelry-making class, since he was making a necklace for her as a surprise anniversary gift.

"Who is it, honey?" Liz asked.

Trying to think fast on her feet, Connie said the first thing she could think of. "I'm Connie Petretta, your neighbor from the seventh floor. I was wondering if you owned a gray BMW. There's a car parked illegally in my spot, and someone told me it might belong to your husband."

"It's not mine," Jerry said. "But I was just leaving. I'll come down and see if I recognize who it belongs to."

Luckily, Liz didn't seem to notice the awkwardness of the conversation. Her eyes were red and puffy, and her gaze seemed distant. Connie

91

wondered if she was upset about what happened to her poetry professor.

"That's nice of you, dear," she said, without making eye contact with either Jerry or Connie.

Jerry kissed his wife, then accompanied Connie to the elevator.

"I apologize," Connie said in a quiet voice, after she heard Liz close the door. "With everything going on, I completely forgot that your wife doesn't know about the class. I came by to make sure you knew about Allister and to ask you a couple of questions."

Connie pressed the elevator call button.

"Look," Jerry said, impatiently staring at the elevator door. "I'm sorry this whole thing is connected to your class, but I don't really have time to talk about what happened to the professor. It's too bad it ended that way for him, but, like I told the police, maybe he flirted with some guy's wife one time too many and paid the price."

"He flirted with *your* wife, didn't he?" Connie asked, looking him in the eyes.

Jerry shifted his weight and checked his watch. "He flirted with anything with a pulse. He thought a lot of himself, but I trust my wife completely."

The elevator finally arrived, and Connie pressed the buttons for the seventh floor for herself and the lobby for Jerry. "Can I ask where you went after class last Thursday?"

"Where did I go? I don't have to tell you what I do with my time. It's not any of your concern."

The elevator door rolled open on Connie's floor. She started to exit the elevator when she heard Jerry let out a deep sigh. So she turned to face him.

"Look, Connie, I don't have anything to hide. I went straight home to an empty house after class. As I told you on Thursday night, my wife was away on business, which is why I was able to keep my surprise and work on the necklace without her knowing about it. Now if you'll excuse me, I have somewhere important to be."

Connie thanked him for his time. "I hope you'll come to the next class to finish your wife's gift," she said.

"I'll be there. Life is too short to sweat the small stuff," he said, as the door closed behind her.

A chill ran through Connie's body. Sweat the small stuff? She didn't consider murder small stuff. They were talking about a human life, after all. And furthermore, Jerry straight up lied to her. She knew from talking with Paige that Jerry went to *Gallagher's* for a beer after class and followed Allister and Paige out of the restaurant.

Unless, of course, Paige had been the one lying, and it *wasn't* Jerry who Ruby heard pounding his fist on his car.

Chapter 9

CONNIE RETURNED TO HER CONDO and tried to shake off her bizarre conversation with Jerry, while she pulled the chicken and potatoes out of the oven and made herself a plate. She didn't learn anything new from talking with him, except that his personality was inconsistent. The Jerry she met tonight was cold-hearted and likely lied about going straight back to Palm Paradise after class. He was a far cry from the man she assisted in lovingly creating an anniversary present for his wife just a few days before.

Since it was too humid to eat on the balcony, Connie set up a TV tray in the air-conditioned living room. She didn't know whether it was because of the heat or the murder investigation, but the chicken landed in her stomach like rocks. She forced down some water, then pushed the tray to the side. Ginger hopped onto her lap, and her big brown eyes pleaded for some chicken.

"How can I say no to that face?" she said, laughing. Connie gave a few pieces to Ginger before storing her leftovers in a container for lunch tomorrow and placing her dish in the dishwasher.

Then she returned to the blue tufted couch, pulled up her feet, and gazed out to the blue waters below.

Even after spending the past few days questioning everyone in her class, Connie was no closer to discovering the murderer's identity. Even though some motives were stronger than others, everyone had at least some reason to want Allister out of the picture. With so many plausible suspects, how was she going to zero in on the real killer?

*   *   *

While having breakfast on Tuesday morning, Connie noticed the ever-growing stack of mail accumulating on her dining room table. Since the mailboxes at Palm Paradise were tiny, she collected her mail nearly every day, but she usually just dumped it on the table. As she sipped her tea, she decided it was as good a time as any to tackle it.

Fortunately, it mostly contained junk mail and bills that she had already paid online. But at the bottom of the pile was a letter from the Board of Trustees, containing minutes from the final meeting of the fiscal year, and a letter informing owners that everything was running smoothly and that the condo fee would not increase this year.

As she glanced at the date of the Trustee meeting and noticed it was the same night that Allister was murdered, she got an idea. If there had been a Trustee meeting that night, then Jessica, the on-site management company employee, would have been working late. Maybe she saw Jerry come in right after class like he said. If she did, that meant he was telling the truth about being at home when Allister was killed and that Paige was the one who was lying. It's possible that it wasn't Jerry who Ruby saw on Thursday night. It was a long shot, and Jessica might not be willing to talk, but maybe she could help Connie at least clear one suspect. Or move Jerry to the top of her list.

Connie took one long sip to finish off her tea, then glanced at her phone to check the time. Jessica would be in at 8:30, which meant that Connie would have just enough time to speak with her and still make it to *Just Jewelry* by 9:00. Since Grace didn't work on Tuesdays, Connie didn't have any wriggle room in her schedule.

After taking a quick shower and loading her car with her laptop and leftovers for lunch, she took Ginger for her morning walk along Sapphire Beach Boulevard, timing her return so it would be just after 8:30, when she was most likely to catch Jessica in her office.

Jessica had just arrived when Connie knocked on the door to her office. She seemed happier to see Ginger than Connie, but Connie couldn't take offense.

"I'm so glad you kept this sweet dog," Jessica said, bending down to scratch the Ginger's head. "She and Concetta were inseparable, and I would miss seeing her around Palm Paradise."

"That was one of the unexpected perks of moving to Sapphire Beach and opening my own shop,"

Connie said. "My life back in Boston wouldn't have permitted me to keep a pet."

"Yes, that reminds me," Jessica said. "I promise I will stop by your shop after work one day. I have heard wonderful things about it. Especially from Gertrude," Jessica added with a chuckle.

"I should put Gertrude on payroll," Connie said. "She saves me a fortune in advertising."

Since Connie didn't have a lot of time, she steered the conversation toward the purpose of her visit. "I finally had a chance to read the minutes from the Trustees meeting on Thursday night."

"Was there a problem with them?" Jessica asked, taking a seat behind her mahogany desk while Connie settled in to one of the black leather chairs facing Jessica. "I thought everyone would be happy that the condo fee will remain the same for the upcoming fiscal year."

"Oh, absolutely," Connie said. "That wasn't what I wanted to talk to you about."

Jessica gave Connie a quizzical look.

"Let me explain. You may have heard about the murder of Allister McCue."

"Yes, the professor over at Florida Sands. What a tragedy."

"Ironically, Allister was a student in my jewelry-making class. He attended class last Thursday just a couple of hours before he was killed." She decided not to mention that her pliers were the murder weapon.

"I'm so sorry, Connie," Jessica said. "That's awful. But I don't see what that has to do with me or the Trustee meeting."

"It's connected in a roundabout way. Since Allister spent the last hours of his life in my store, and was a valued student, I have been asking around a little bit, trying to get to the bottom of what happened."

Jessica smiled and playfully shook her head. "Of course you have. You can't seem to stay away from a mystery, can you?"

Connie looked thoughtfully at Jessica. "I wouldn't put it that way. It's more like *they* can't stay away from *me*."

"Fair enough," Jessica said. "But I still don't see what this has to do with the meeting."

"You may have some information that can help me," Connie said. "Jerry Morrison in 1010 was also a student in my class. By the way, don't mention it in front of his wife, because he is taking the class in secret to make her a necklace for their upcoming anniversary."

Jessica made a motion with her fingers, signifying that she was locking her lips and throwing away the key.

"Anyway, Jerry clearly disliked Allister for reasons it's not worth getting into now."

Jessica didn't press Connie for a reason.

"But since you were here late that night for the meeting, I was wondering if you saw him return home, and if so, what time it was. Jerry told me that he came straight home from my class, but I don't think he did."

Jessica nodded and appeared to be thinking about it. "I do agree with you that Jerry hasn't been himself lately. He has been visibly preoccupied. But I don't think I'm comfortable spying on residents, especially in their home. The lobby is part of Palm Paradise, and we want everyone to feel like it's an extension of their home."

Connie had been afraid Jessica was going to take that position, but she thought she'd give it one last attempt. "It isn't exactly spying. It's not like you were hiding in your office and eavesdropping on conversations. It's just that you have a clear view of the lobby from here," Connie said, turning around to point at the floor to ceiling windows that made up the wall between Jessica's office and the lobby. "And this information could point me in the right direction. If you saw Jerry come home right after class, then I would know he is innocent. But if not, it's at least worth investigating."

Jessica appeared to consider the situation. "Well, you *were* helpful in solving those murderers back in January..."

"Helpful?" Connie said, pretending to be insulted. "I single-handedly solved them. Palm Paradise owes me this favor."

Jessica raised her palms toward Connie. "Okay, you're very convincing. I left Palm Paradise really late last Thursday. I rarely work that late, but the Trustees meeting got postponed a couple of times, so they didn't meet until the very end of June. I wanted to get the minutes typed up and the letter written, so we could get it into residents' mailboxes the next morning. Jerry was just getting home as I was leaving Palm Paradise - about 11:30 on Thursday night. He looked disheveled and upset about something. I tried to ask him how he was, but he just grunted and walked straight past me." Jessica let out a deep sigh. "I certainly hope Jerry is not the killer. Palm Paradise doesn't need any more bad publicity after what happened in January."

Connie couldn't disagree with that.

Chapter 10

AFTER HER CONVERSATION with Jessica, Connie arrived at work without a minute to spare and opened the shop at 9:00 sharp. She was prepared for a slow day, since the weather app on her phone indicated that the temperature would reach the mid-nineties with high humidity and a threat of thunder showers throughout the day. Typical southwest Florida weather for the month of July. She decided to take a break from the sapphire-blue necklace she had been working on and to spend the day making some earrings. They would provide a nice break from the more involved necklace.

Throughout the morning, she made solid progress creating three pairs of earrings with extra beads that she had on hand, in between posting on social media and waiting on the occasional customer. By late morning, she was ready for a break, so she poured herself some iced tea and stood by one of her display windows watching the bathing-suit-clad passersby carrying coolers, umbrellas, and beach bags on their way to enjoy a day in the sun.

Behind a group of beachgoers, Connie spotted Gallagher heading toward his restaurant. When he saw Connie standing in the window, he shifted his direction and came into Connie's shop.

"It looks like it's going to be a slow day downtown," he said with a friendly smile.

"I think you're right. Although I can't say I mind all that much. I could use a quiet day to make some jewelry. I'm trying to fill my storage room with product during the summer months to be ready for the return of the snowbirds and tourists."

"Sounds like good planning."

Connie led him to the seating area and offered him an iced tea.

"No thanks. I can't stay long, but I will sit down for a few minutes."

Connie got a bottle of water from the fridge. "At least take this. I'm finding it's nearly impossible stay well-hydrated this time of year."

He smiled and accepted the water. "Say, I've been meaning to ask you how your investigating is going."

Connie shrugged. "Not that great. Basically, everyone who was in my class on Thursday night, except for my friends, of course, seem to have some type of motive and no alibi. I do have my suspicions, but you can't take suspicions to the police. I would need something more solid before talking to Josh or Zach."

"Like evidence, you mean? Yeah, those darn police detectives are sticklers for evidence," he said with a playful smile.

There was something about Gallagher's demeanor that always managed to bring a smile to Connie's face. He had a way about him that made it easy for her to relax and be herself.

"What about the young woman who the victim was hitting on in my restaurant?" he asked.

"That was Paige. She's a graduate student and was Allister's teaching assistant. She is still on my list, but it turns out he wasn't trying to date her. He was trying to get into her good graces, because he was dating her mother."

"Interesting. But still, she seemed to dislike him. A lot."

"That's why she's still on my list. Who knows how far she might have gone if she felt she needed to protect her mother? But my biggest suspect at this point is a guy named Jerry Morrison from Palm Paradise." Connie told Gallagher about Jerry's behavior in and after class, what Mary Ann said about his confrontation with Allister while dropping his wife off for class, and her experience talking with him the night before. "Even Jessica, the condo management employee at Palm Paradise, agreed that he has seemed out of sorts lately. And she saw him return home late Thursday night, which would have given him enough time to commit the murder."

"Hmmm, sounds like a definite possibility."

"Gallagher," Connie said, snapping her fingers as she remembered something she wanted to ask him. "Paige claimed that Jerry was at your bar while she and Allister were eating last Thursday, and that Jerry left right behind them. She said he followed them out of the restaurant. Do you happen to remember seeing him? He's probably in his mid-fifties, medium build with brown hair, graying around his temples."

Gallagher narrowed his eyes and looked toward the ceiling. "I remember that the bar was busy that night, so I was backing up my bartender. There was a guy who fits that description sitting at the bar. I remember him, because he was staring at his glass of beer and looked to be a million miles away. I sometimes try to make small talk with customers, but this guy clearly didn't want any part of a conversation, so I left him alone."

"That could be him. Would he have been able to see Allister and Paige from where he was sitting?"

"He was seated at the far end of the bar, so yes, he could easily have seen them. But honestly, I don't know if he left at the same time as Paige and Allister. I went out back to get another keg for the bartender but got sidetracked with a phone call. When I returned, all three were gone, so I can't say if they left together."

This information kept Jerry on the top of Connie's list. Between what Jessica, Ruby, Mary Ann, and Gallagher all said, Connie was more inclined to believe Paige than Jerry at this point.

Gallagher finished off his water with one last long sip and stood to leave. "I'd better get over there," he said, pointing to his restaurant across the street.

Connie loved the exotic feel his thatched roof gave to her view.

"By the way, thanks for the invite to the fireworks on the Fourth of July, but I'll have to take a rain check. It'll be a madhouse at my restaurant."

"I figured that. I just wanted you and Penelope to know you are both welcome. Hopefully, we can all do something together after hours another time."

"Definitely."

Connie watched Gallagher cross the street and climb the wooden stairs that led into his restaurant, then returned to the table to work on more earrings.

The rest of Tuesday and Wednesday were slow, undoubtedly due to the sporadic thunder showers that pelted the area. Connie was glad she insisted that Grace take the day off. Although she would have enjoyed the company, there wouldn't have been much for Grace to do besides people watch with Connie. As soon as the dark clouds rolled in, like clockwork, folks would scurry out of the shops and off the beach, racing to their cars for cover. Connie lost more than a couple of customers to the sound of crashing thunder that seemed to precede the violent rainstorms.

On Wednesday afternoon, she queued up a few days' worth of social media posts on various outlets, including a slew of posts advertising a Fourth of July sale she decided to have at the last minute, in hopes of drawing into her store some of the crowd that would be at the beach for the festivities the following day.

Connie glanced at the clouds in the distance slowly rolling in and decided to take Ginger for a walk before it began to rain. Since she planned to stay within view of the store in case any customers came around, she didn't bother hanging a sign to indicate that she would return shortly.

Connie locked the door, and she and Ginger strolled down the street in the direction of the beach. As they were turning around to come back, Emily, the owner of *Friendly Scoops*, was sitting on a bench in front of her store and motioned for Connie to come over.

Connie glanced back at *Just Jewelry,* then at Emily. If she went over, she wouldn't be able to see if any customers were looking for her. But then again, it had been so slow all day. A short delay shouldn't hurt.

Ginger was her usual charming self, hopping onto the bench between the two women and lapping up the attention that Emily gave her. Connie and Emily chatted for a few minutes about all things Sapphire Beach before Connie excused herself to get back to the shop.

As they got close to the store, Ginger slowed her pace and raised her ears. Connie pulled her along, but the dog resisted. She picked her up, but something felt off kilter. When Connie inserted her key in the lock, she discovered the reason. The door was unlocked. *What on earth?* She remembered locking it with one-hundred-percent certainty. Connie hadn't enabled the alarm, since she wasn't going far, but she definitely locked the door.

Connie cautiously peeked her head inside, but the store appeared to be empty and her merchandise was all intact.

Burglars didn't usually come in the middle of the day, anyway.

Connie started toward the checkout area, located in the middle of the store, to inspect the cash register when she heard a noise out back.

As she grabbed a pair of pliers from her jewelry-making tool kit, she didn't know if she was more afraid for her own safety, or that her pliers would once again become a lethal weapon as she tiptoed toward the back of the store.

Before any harm could be done, a man and a woman casually wandered out.

It was her landlord, Mickey Miranda, and his wife, Susan.

Susan let out a loud squeal when she saw Connie's pliers raised above her head while Mickey jumped in front of his wife.

Connie lowered the pliers and breathed a sigh of relief. "You guys scared me half to death. What are you doing in here?" She hoped Mickey's surprise visit wasn't connected to Allister's death, or to the fact that her pliers were used as a murder weapon. If that were the case, Connie defending herself with pliers probably didn't bode well.

Mickey ran his hand through his hair. "Connie, I was so worried about you after what happened at the pier last week. Susan and I were visiting our daughter in New Jersey. We just flew home this morning and heard what happened. When nobody was here in the middle of the day, I figured something must be wrong and let myself in."

After Connie explained where she had been, Susan left Connie and Mickey to talk while she browsed the Fair Trade section, stopping to read the biographies of the artisans.

But Mickey didn't give Connie a chance to say anything. Shifting nervously, he blurted out, "I assume you heard about the murder that took place by the pier. I just wanted you to know that the police are doing everything they can to catch the killer, and they don't believe that anyone in the area is in danger. I wanted to reassure you, after everything that happened with Natasha, that you are safe in your own shop." Natasha was the shop's previous tenant who had disappeared without a trace. Connie was instrumental in uncovering what happened to her.

Connie felt her shoulders relax. Mickey didn't think she was a jinx. He wasn't looking to throw her out of his building. He was genuinely concerned for her safety.

Susan held up a necklace made by one of Connie's Kenyan artisans. "Is the Fourth of July sale in effect yet?"

Connie assured her that it was, and Susan brought the necklace to the circular checkout counter.

It occurred to Connie that since Mickey had just spoken to the police about the investigation, maybe he knew something. "Do you know if the police are close to making an arrest?" she asked, wrapping Susan's necklace and placing it in a bag.

"As of late this morning, they were not. But Detective Josh Miller told me that the preliminary autopsy report was back, and it confirmed that the time of death was indeed around 11:00 PM, as the police initially suspected." Mickey puffed out his chest. "He didn't want to give that information, but I told him that I have tenants who work nearby and wanted to be sure they weren't in any danger."

"You take good care of us, Mickey. It's nice to know you have our backs."

He waved at her and winked as they were leaving, and Connie couldn't help but laugh.

What started out as a boring day turned unexpectedly, and unnecessarily, eventful.

Chapter 11

ON THE MORNING of the Fourth of July, Connie awoke before her phone alarm sounded, eager for a busy day in the shop and a fun evening with friends watching fireworks on the beach after hours.

"Come on, Ginger, I hope you'll do okay with the noise and the crowds today," Connie said as she nudged the dog into her Jetta. She thought of leaving Ginger behind, further away from the noisy fireworks, but with the traffic to and from the beach, which was sure to make Sapphire Beach Boulevard nearly impassible, she feared she wouldn't be able to get home in the afternoon to walk and feed her.

Connie glanced up at Palm Paradise as she exited the underground parking garage and thought of her balcony overlooking the beach, where she and her friends could have enjoyed a prime view of the fireworks. She was somewhat disappointed at not being able to watch the festivities from her balcony, but at least she would be in the middle of the action. Maybe another year.

She took a right on Sapphire Beach Boulevard and swung by *Sweet Dreams*, the only bakery in town, to pick up the pastry order for her gathering that evening, then stopped at Publix for a few extra cases of water. It was sure to be a scorcher. With the necessary supplies loaded into her backseat, Connie doubled back down the boulevard, arriving at her shop well before traffic could slow her down.

In all the years Connie visited her Aunt Concetta, she had never spent a Fourth of July in Sapphire Beach. In fact, since it was so hot this time of year, Concetta often would spend the month of July in Boston. So, she wasn't sure exactly what to expect, especially in terms of traffic in her store.

Grace, who fortunately insisted on working that day, even though Thursday was supposed to be one of her days off, arrived in the shop shortly after Connie.

"I'll be curious to see how much jewelry we sell today," Grace said, nodding with satisfaction at the store, which was sparkling clean and ready for customers. "I know there will be tons of people downtown, but I'm not sure how many will be in a shopping mood."

By 11:00, parking lots were filling up and the downtown streets were bustling with activity. Connie glanced over at *Gallagher's Tropical Shack* and was pleased to see that there was already a long stream of customers filing in. Gallagher poured his heart and soul into his restaurant and, in Connie's humble opinion, he deserved all the success in the world.

The consistently large volume of customers meant that Connie and Grace were on their feet all day and barely found a moment to sneak out back, one at a time, to wolf down a sandwich. It was a good problem to have, but by the end of the day, Connie desperately needed to get off her feet.

By the time her friends arrived at 7:30, customers were making their way out of the shops and into restaurants or down to the beach to claim a spot to watch the fireworks that were scheduled to take place at 9:30. She quickly looked over the credit card receipts in her cash register and was pleasantly surprised at the amount of business she did. It was a welcome boost in revenue in the middle of a relatively slow season. And the sale succeeded in drawing lots of traffic into her store. She would certainly be doing this again next year.

Elyse and Stephanie helped Connie brew some coffee and put the pastry out for her guests on the oak table, which, this evening, felt more like a dining room table than a jewelry-making station. Everyone gathered around, including Emma and Victoria. It was the first time her friends had been together in the shop all at once since her grand opening nearly three months before.

Although things were far from normal with Zach, he did seem to relax a little. Perhaps he realized that Connie was stepping back to give him the space he apparently needed. The comfortable, easy feeling that Connie had always felt in his presence had greatly diminished, but she tried not to let it bring her down. If Zach only wanted to be friends, she just wished he'd say so. She didn't want any awkwardness between them to make her or the others uncomfortable. For now, she would try to put it aside and enjoy the evening.

Fortunately, there was plenty to distract her. Victoria melted Connie's heart when she looked up at her in her little Fourth of July sundress, complete with red sunglasses and flip flops, asking for a "patry". Connie scooped the child up onto her lap, where she enjoyed an éclair, the biggest piece of pastry in the box, and proceeded to get more cream and frosting on her hands and face than in her mouth. After Victoria polished off the last bite, Connie brought her out back to clean her up. Once she returned a squeaky-clean Victoria to her parents, Elyse and Josh updated the group on the adoption process.

"It's been about three months since we began the process," Josh said. They had announced their plans to adopt Victoria at that very same table at the grand opening of *Just Jewelry* in April. "We hired a fantastic attorney who is trying to move things along as quickly as possible. He tells us that if all continues to go smoothly, she should officially be our daughter in another three to six months."

"But as far as we're concerned, she is already our daughter," Elyse said, kissing the blond little girl's chubby cheeks. Judging from her grin, Victoria obviously felt the same way.

But Connie wasn't so sure that Emma did. She couldn't help but notice the sense of betrayal in Emma's eyes as her parents doted on the newest addition to their family.

Connie and Stephanie went out back to bring out more coffee, and when they returned, Gertrude was asking Josh and Zach about their progress on the murder investigation.

"I've been wondering about the investigation myself," Connie said, pouring herself another cup. It had been a tiring day on her feet, and she needed a boost of energy to enjoy the fireworks. "I don't know what I'm going to do about my jewelry-making class."

Josh shook his head playfully. "Connie, how is it that you always end up in the middle of our murder investigations?"

"I think you have it all wrong, my friend. I don't get in the middle of *your* investigations; your investigations seem to barge their way into *my* life. This never happened back home."

Elyse put a protective arm around Connie's shoulders. "Leave her alone. She's stressed out enough about the fact that her first class ended in murder."

"Not to mention that my favorite pliers were used as a murder weapon. I'm counting on you two to get this figured out before people start associating *Just Jewelry* with homicide," Connie said.

"Poor Allister," Gertrude said. "He was a little snooty for my taste, but nobody deserves what happened to him."

"His colleagues from the university said he was quite the literature snob," Grace said. "He would criticize any books that didn't meet his high standards."

Josh and Zach exchanged a humorous glance, both trying unsuccessfully to suppress a smirk.

"What's so funny?" Elyse asked.

Zach took a sip of coffee, then pushed his cup away. "Allister McCue was no literature snob. He may have insulted what he deemed 'trashy novels' in public, but we found copies of some pretty sappy stuff hidden in his desk drawer. Whatever he said in front of his colleagues, privately it was a different story. Literally."

Gertrude's eyes flew wide open. "What kind of books did you find in his drawer?" she asked.

"They couldn't have been *that* bad," Stephanie said.

"*A Professor's Fantasy. A Campus Affair.* I can't even remember the rest, but they were pretty bad," Josh said.

"No way!" Connie said.

Everyone laughed, including Emma. Even Victoria joined in, apparently not wanting to be left out of all the fun.

"Well, I guess everyone's entitled to their secrets," Connie said. "But I wonder why he made such a big deal about putting the stuff down. Clearly the others in the department didn't share his disdain for it. They were even talking about a romance novel at the jewelry-making class."

Connie looked over at Emma and noticed she wore a sour expression on her face.

"Is something wrong, Emma?" Connie asked. "Don't you like your cannoli?"

She put down the pastry on the paper plate in front of her and pushed it away. "It's not that. I just don't understand why Victoria is laughing. She doesn't even understand why it's funny. She throws herself into the middle of everything we do."

Josh tried to reason with her. "Honey, Victoria is your sister. It's natural for her to want to do everything we do. You should take it as a compliment."

"I liked it better before she came," Emma said, hitting the table with her hand.

"You don't mean that, sweetie," Gertrude said.

"I'm sorry, it's just that she's *always* here. She never leaves us alone. I miss the old days when it was just the three of us."

Connie's heart broke when she saw the pain on Elyse's face.

Emma looked at Victoria with disdain. "Can I go play with Ginger out back?"

Elyse nodded. "Go ahead, honey."

After Emma was out of earshot, Elyse confided to the others that she didn't know what to do about Emma. "At first she was so excited about having a little sister, but now she seems over it. I think it's

125

starting to sink in what a big a change it is for our family. Maybe we didn't properly prepare her."

"You can't blame yourself, honey. Just give her some time," Grace said. "She'll adapt. It's a tough adjustment at any age."

"I hope you're right," Elyse said. But she didn't look convinced.

After putting aside what was left of the pastry and throwing away the paper dishes and cups, some of the group moved over to the seating area while others lingered at the table.

When lingering shoppers trickled in here and there, Connie excused herself to wait on them and offered them some pastry after ringing up their purchases. At 9:00, Connie locked up the shop, and the group made their way to the beach.

"Look, there's some room over there," Emma said, pointing to a spot a short distance from the pier, where the festivities would take place.

"It's as good a spot as any," Josh said.

As they passed underneath the weather-beaten wooden pier, Connie tried not to think of Allister being killed with her pliers in that very spot, but she couldn't help it. She glanced at the ground, half-hoping to find a clue, but she knew that would be impossible. The tide had come in and out more than a dozen times since last week. Her expression must have given away her thoughts. Josh had walked up alongside her and gave her a knowing glance.

"Let's try not to think about it tonight," he said with a warm smile.

Connie nodded. "I'll try."

It turned out to be easier than she thought. Excitement floated in the air as people of all ages anxiously anticipated the fireworks display. The air was still hot even though the sun had set, but there was a consistent breeze coming off the Gulf, which made the heat and humidity bearable.

Zach had stuck pretty close to Josh for most of the night, but while they waited for the fireworks to begin, Connie and Zach shared a blanket, with Ginger sitting between them.

"How are things going, Zach? Is work busy these days?"

He flashed her an easy smile. "Things are busy, but nothing we can't manage." He gave Ginger a little attention, then said, "I've had a lot on my mind lately."

As soon as the words came out of his mouth, Zach seemed to regret saying them.

"Anything in particular?" Connie ventured.

Zach shifted uncomfortably on the blanket and changed the subject without answering Connie's question, asking her how business had been since the grand opening. It was an awkward transition, but Connie went with it, filling him in on the ups and downs of the past few months.

The spectacular light show above the Gulf of Mexico started right on time. There was something magical about fireworks on the Fourth of July that closed the gap between time and space. As an array of colors exploded in the sky, Connie recollected so many other Fourth of July celebrations she had attended over her thirty-four years of life. She was glad to be sharing this one with her new Sapphire Beach friends, who had become as close as family in some ways. She hoped and prayed that, one day soon, her family would visit and all her loved ones would be sitting together on the beach or around her dining room table.

Chapter 12

AROUND MID-MORNING on Friday, Connie and Grace had just taken down the "Fourth of July Sale" signs and gotten the store back in order from the activities of the previous day when Gertrude popped in for an unexpected visit.

Gertrude dropped her purse onto the table and Connie went over to greet her. But before Connie could open her mouth, Gertrude gripped Connie's forearm and blurted out, "You aren't going to believe what happened."

"Hello, Gertrude. What a pleasant surprise," Grace said, joining the two women. "Can I get you an iced tea?"

Gertrude shook her head back and forth. "No, thank you. I just came by to tell you the news in person."

Connie led her to the sofa, and she and Grace took the two armchairs facing Gertrude.

Grace tried to make small talk about the fireworks the night before, but Gertrude wanted no part of that. She was a woman on a mission.

"It's Jerry," she said. "He died Tuesday morning."

"Jerry Morrison?" Grace asked with wide eyes.

"From my jewelry-making class?" Connie echoed. As far as she knew he wasn't sick, and she hadn't heard anything on the news about a fatal accident lately. Of course, she had been quite absorbed in work the past few days. But still. Josh or Zach would have mentioned it last night. Wouldn't they?

"Yes, some of our neighbors were talking about it in the lobby of Palm Paradise. They informed me that his wake is tonight at the Anderson-Bradley Funeral Home. Elyse and I are planning to pay our respects. She sold Jerry and Liz their condo several years ago. You're welcome to come with us if you'd like."

Connie placed her hand on top of her head and struggled to process the information. "I don't understand. I just talked to him on Monday night." She remembered how peculiarly he was acting and wondered if there was a connection between his abrupt behavior and a possible health condition. Sometimes people got short-tempered when they were ill. "He didn't seem sick at all. Do you know how he died?"

Gertrude shrugged her shoulders. "They didn't say. I just caught the tail end of the conversation and got the information about his services."

"It could have been a massive heart attack, or an aneurism or something like that," Grace said. "That's usually how people die unexpectedly. Unless of course drugs were involved. That could explain his inconsistent behavior," she added.

"I guess it could be any of those things," Connie said. Then, turning to Elyse and Gertrude, she added, "I'd like to come to the wake with you since Jerry was my student. I only met him a couple of times, but I'd like to offer my condolences to Liz and tell her about the necklace he was making for her."

"I'll cover the store for you," Grace said. "Please offer Liz my sympathies and explain why I couldn't be there."

"Grace, the funeral home is just a few minutes away. Since they were your neighbors, why don't you close the shop for a few minutes around dinner time and come by briefly to pay your respects? You can put the sign up that says, 'Be back in five minutes.' I doubt anyone will miss you."

"I think I'll do that," Grace said. "We did live in the same building, and Palm Paradise *is* like a tight little neighborhood." Grace shook her head, as if the news was just sinking in. "Poor Liz. She must be devastated. I'll make a casserole for her this weekend and bring it to her."

"It's settled then," Gertrude said to Connie. "Elyse and I will pick you up here at 4:00."

***

Elyse and Gertrude arrived right on time, and by 4:20, they were at the Anderson-Bradley Funeral Home, just outside Sapphire Beach. In addition to paying her respects, Connie was anxious to learn everything she could about Jerry. He had been her prime suspect in Allister's murder, and just because he died unexpectedly didn't mean he was innocent. It wasn't, of course, that she wanted to tarnish his reputation. She just wanted to know if there was still a murderer in her class.

Gertrude was all for doing a little sleuthing, and she and Connie agreed on a plan of attack. After they paid their respects, they would divide up the room and casually see what they could learn about Jerry from his friends, family, and acquaintances.

Elyse went on the record as saying that their plan went against her better judgment, but there wasn't much she could do, since she was outnumbered.

The three women signed the guest book as soon as they arrived, then got in line to say a prayer at the coffin and offer their condolences to Jerry's loved ones. They were holding it together surprisingly well for having unexpectedly lost a loved one. Connie almost felt guilty for thinking it, but maybe it was because they grew tired of his Jekyll-and-Hyde personality.

As she waited for Elyse and Gertrude to finish making their way through the line, Connie scanned the room. She didn't recognize anyone, except a few familiar faces from Palm Paradise.

Not seeing Liz Morrison in the receiving line, Connie searched the room for her. She at least wanted to tell her about the necklace Jerry had been making for her as a surprise anniversary gift. *Perhaps she is in the restroom,* Connie thought. *Or talking with guests in another room.*

Elyse and Gertrude rejoined Connie, and the three women stepped into an adjoining room, where several poster boards containing a photo collage of Jerry and his loved ones were displayed on easels.

As they entered the room, Gertrude pointed out Jerry's son, who was talking with another man. He was wearing a black polo shirt and khaki pants.

"How rude," Gertrude said, a little too loudly for Connie's comfort.

Elyse put her finger to her lips, and, catching her signal, Gertrude lowered her voice an octave. But the indignant expression was still plastered on her face. "You would think the man would at least wear a suit to his father's wake."

Elyse shrugged. "To each his own, I guess."

Gertrude introduced Connie to some Palm Paradise residents while Elyse perused the photo display. Elyse's eyes narrowed in confusion as she looked at Connie, then back at the photos. She eventually rejoined Gertrude and Connie, but the same puzzled look remained on her face.

"Something seems strange," Elyse said. "Jerry doesn't look like himself in those photos. I mean, they kind of look like him, but not exactly."

"Believe me," Gertrude said, "people change over the years. I'm living proof of that."

"Aren't we all?" Connie asked.

"I guess," Elyse said.

Just as the words left Elyse's mouth, Jerry and Liz solemnly walked out from the funeral director's office and toward the viewing room.

Gertrude's jaw dropped to the ground, and her eyes flew wide open as she watched them speak to a woman in a black dress standing near the casket. "Whooooah," Gertrude said, appearing unsteady on her feet.

As Elyse and Connie each grabbed one of Gertrude's elbows to support her, they exchanged a confused look.

135

"Um, Aunt Gertrude," Elyse said, slowly and deliberately, "are you sure your friends said that *Jerry* Morrison passed away?"

"He's clearly *not* dead," Connie said, her eyes glued on Jerry and Liz.

"Doesn't Jerry have a brother?" Elyse whispered.

Connie glanced around the room to make sure nobody could hear them. It was bad enough that their jaws were still hanging on the ground. She would be mortified if anyone realized the mistake they just made.

Recovering from her initial shock, Gertrude slapped her palm against her forehead. "Yes, you're right, dear. Jerry had a brother named Jesse. It's all coming back to me now. I met him in the elevator a few times when he would visit Jerry. You know, they looked so darned much alike, I would always confuse the two when Jesse visited. It must be *Jesse* who died."

Elyse shook her head back and forth, unable to suppress a smirk. "That would explain why Jerry doesn't look like himself in the photos. He *isn't* himself."

"And why Liz wasn't in the receiving line," Connie said.

"And why Jerry's son is not wearing a suit." Elyse added. "It's not his father's wake. It's his uncle's."

"I still say he should have worn a suit," Gertrude said, trying against all hope to save face. But as the magnitude of her mistake apparently sunk in, she hung her head in shame. "I'm so sorry that I wasted your evening, ladies. I feel so foolish."

Connie put an arm around Gertrude's shoulders and gave them a squeeze. "Don't you worry, Gertrude. It could have happened to anyone." Connie met Elyse's disbelieving stare and shrugged her shoulders. She wasn't sure what else to say to make Gertrude feel better.

"On a more positive note," Gertrude said, "I guess this means that your prime suspect is still alive. It will make your investigation easier."

Connie was about to respond when Jerry approached them.

"Ladies, it's so kind of you to come to my brother's wake," he said. "Did you know Jesse well?"

Elyse thought quickly. "Actually, we didn't. Connie and I accompanied my Aunt Gertrude."

Connie hoped Jerry wouldn't realize that Gertrude had only met Jesse in passing. "We also wanted to offer you our deepest sympathies on the passing of your brother. It must be a difficult time for you," Connie added.

Tears threatened to spill from Jerry's eyes, so Connie took a tissue from a box on a nearby end table and handed it to him.

"That's kind of you," he said, clutching the tissue. "I'm glad you came. It gives me the chance to apologize to you for my abrupt behavior when you stopped by on Monday night. I was on my way to the hospital to visit my brother, and I knew it might be one of the last times I saw him."

"There's no need to apologize," Connie said, placing a hand on his elbow. "You had a lot going on." She felt a twinge of guilt for assuming the worst about Jerry. No wonder his behavior had been erratic. His brother was dying. Connie couldn't even imagine how she would behave if she were going through something similar with her sister.

"Yes, that's true, but it's no excuse. I also wanted you to know that the reason I avoided your question when you asked me where I was after class last Thursday is because I was visiting my brother that night. Actually, I stopped at *Gallagher's* for a quick beer, then spent the next couple of hours at the hospital."

He wiped his eyes with the tissue.

"You see, Jesse was very sick for the past year, and he wanted privacy during his illness. So, to respect his wishes, I wasn't able to tell anyone where I was. I didn't even tell the police, since Jesse was friends with some members of the police department. He just didn't want anyone seeing him so sick, and he knew people would insist on visiting if they knew his situation. He was a proud man, and I didn't necessarily agree with his decision, but I had to respect my brother's request. I know it must have looked bad. I'll straighten things out with the police in a couple of days, after the funeral. There are a number of hospital workers, as well as my sister, who can vouch for my whereabouts last Thursday evening."

Chapter 13

JERRY POLITELY EXCUSED himself and returned to his family's side.

"I guess you can cross Jerry off your list of suspects," Elyse said.

"At least it wasn't a total waste of an evening," Gertrude said, still trying to find a bright side to the whole situation.

"That reminds me. I'd better text Grace and tell her not to bother to come," Connie said.

She pulled her phone from her purse and shot Grace a brief text, but unfortunately it was too late. As soon as Connie hit "send," Grace walked into the funeral home. She gave a slight wave upon spotting Connie, Elyse, and Gertrude, then continued resolutely toward the casket to pay her respects.

Gertrude followed her and tried to lead her away from the viewing room, but Grace insisted that she didn't have any time to spare. "I can't leave the shop unattended for long. I only have time to say a quick prayer and offer my condolences, then I need to get right back to *Just Jewelry*."

Connie stood frozen as she watched the conversation between Gertrude and Grace from a short distance away. If Grace went into that room and saw Jerry, who knows how that would end? She had visions of Grace fainting or shrieking.

After what seemed like an eternity, Gertrude finally won out. She grabbed her arm and managed to pull an annoyed Grace away from the viewing room and over to Connie and Elyse.

Connie breathed a sigh of relief.

"Before you go into that room, there's something you need to know," Gertrude said. "Jerry's in there."

"Of course Jerry's in there!" Grace said, trying to break free from Gertrude's grip and head back toward the casket. "I was just going over to his coffin to say a prayer."

"No, no, no," Gertrude said. "Jerry is *alive*. We had the wrong dead guy."

Connie looked around to make sure nobody could overhear them. Seeing a couple of turned heads, she motioned for Gertrude and Grace to lower their voices.

"The wrong *what*?" Grace asked.

Grace looked to Connie and Elyse for some type of clarification.

"She's right. We had the wrong dead guy," Connie said, unable to think of another way to phrase it.

Connie and Elyse proceeded to tell the entire story to Grace, including their conversation with Jerry where he revealed his alibi for the night of Allister's murder.

"Well," Grace said quietly, trying not to draw any more attention to their little group, "you certainly had an interesting evening, didn't you?"

Connie noticed the sides of Grace's mouth turning upward. She looked away from Grace so she wouldn't start laughing. If she started to laugh, she was afraid she wouldn't be able to stop.

"It's all my fault," Gertrude said. "I misunderstood the women talking at Palm Paradise. Jerry. Jesse. They both sound alike."

"It wasn't a total waste," Grace said, suppressing her smile and attempting to console Gertrude. "At least Connie can cross Jerry off her list of suspects."

"Absolutely," Connie said. "In fact, you did me a favor. We learned a lot tonight. It was well worth the trip."

"Well," Grace said, shrugging her shoulders and turning her palms upward, "I might as well say a quick prayer for Jesse, anyway, and offer my sympathies while I'm here. After all, a man still died. But thank you for sparing me the shock of coming face to face with Jerry."

Connie decided to ride back to *Just Jewelry* with Grace, so Gertrude and Elyse left while Grace went through the receiving line.

"You might as well take the rest of the evening off," Connie said, as they were driving back. "Maybe you can still salvage what's left of it."

"Don't you worry about my evening," Grace said, giving in to laughter as the evening's events fully sank in. She slapped the top of her thigh. "That's the funniest thing that's happened to me in a long while. The comic relief alone is worth giving up a few hours off."

Grace's laughter was contagious. By the time they arrived at the shop, Connie's cheeks were sore. But she had to admit a good belly laugh was just what she needed to melt away some of the stress of the past seven days.

Grace came into *Just Jewelry* to get a bag that she left in the store, and as she was about to leave, the door chimed. It was Elyse.

"I was planning on staying at the wake a lot longer, so after I dropped Aunt Gertrude off, I thought I'd come by for a visit. Josh is home with the girls, so I might as well take advantage of a free evening."

"In that case, I'll stay for a few more minutes," Grace said.

Connie poured them each some pineapple juice, which she had made fresh with her juicer that morning, and brought it to the sofa area, where the others were relaxing.

"I can honestly say that tonight was a first for me," Grace said. "In all my years, I have never been to a wake for the wrong person."

"Poor Gertrude," Elyse said. "I don't know if she'll ever be able to look Jerry in the face again.

Even though he has absolutely no idea what happened."

"All in all, it was a productive evening, though," Connie said. "Until Jerry revealed his alibi, he was my top suspect."

"So, who else is left on your list?" Elyse asked.

Connie leaned her elbow on the back of the sofa and rested the side of her head on her hand. "I still haven't ruled out Abby or Paige. Abby stood to gain a lot from Allister's death. She had a lifelong dream of becoming a writer and professor, and if he had turned her in for plagiarism, it would have created a major obstacle in achieving it. And Paige clearly hated Allister because he was dating her mother."

"I remember the tension between them at the jewelry-making class," Elyse said.

"And didn't you say that Paige and Allister had dinner at *Gallagher's*?" Grace asked.

"Yes. Paige may have been the last person to see Allister alive. She claims that Allister was talking with Jerry when she drove away, but if she is the killer, she's not going to admit to being alone with him at the end of the evening,"

"She could easily have pretended to drive away and then followed him to the beach and killed him," Elyse said.

"Allister's murder had to have been premeditated, because whoever killed him stole my pliers to use as a murder weapon. But if Allister followed Paige into *Gallagher's*, as Paige claims, she couldn't have been planning his death, because she couldn't have known that Allister would follow her."

"Again, unless she was lying," Elyse said. "Maybe she invited him to meet her there and made it look like he followed her."

"Right. Either Paige is blatantly lying, or she is innocent," Connie said.

Connie downed her last sip of pineapple juice. "Or it could have been Isabel or Mary Ann. They both had motives, as well, and access to the pliers. Abby thinks that Isabel was afraid that Allister was after her job, now that he had tenure. It seems she voted against him. And, according to Abby, Allister was less than kind to Mary Ann at work. She also said that Mary Ann and Allister had a falling out, but she didn't know all the details.

"Unless Abby's making up stories to save herself," Grace said.

"Could be. One thing is for certain. Now that we know that Jerry is innocent, the killer has to be someone from the Florida Sands group." Connie stroked her chin. "I need to find a way to talk to them again."

"How are you going to manage that?" Elyse asked.

She thought about inviting the class back for a tutoring session, but with the increased workload in the English Department, she doubted that anyone would come.

"I'm still working on that."

Chapter 14

CONNIE SET HER ALARM for early Saturday morning so she could go for a paddle before work. Until she hired another employee at *Just Jewelry*, mornings would be her only opportunity to enjoy the outdoors. Which worked out okay since, this time of year, the afternoon sun was oppressively hot. Grace would be in the shop by 9:00, so if Connie was running a few minutes late, it would be no big deal.

She went down to the underground garage to get her powder-blue paddleboard, paddle, and matching lifejacket from her storage unit, attached the board to the dolly, and wheeled it down to the beach. It was a calm morning, which bode well for Connie. Although she had taken her board out regularly since she bought it in March, she was by no means an expert. She had mastered the art of turning and could even navigate some of the waves that came her way from speedboats and jet skis without immediately tumbling into the water, but that was about the extent of her skill set. Not that falling into the warm, blue-green waters of the Gulf of Mexico was the worst thing in the world. A dunk in the water, intentional or unintentional, provided a welcome relief from the scorching sun.

Leaving her dolly, towel, and cover-up on the beach, Connie fastened her lifejacket and dragged her paddleboard into the water. She knelt on the board and paddled out into deeper waters, then stood up like a boss. A smile immediately came to her face as the warm breeze pushed back her shoulder-length dark hair. Fortunately, Connie's olive skin meant that it took longer for her to get sunburnt.

The water was refreshing as it splashed on her legs while she rhythmically paddled her way along the coastline. She usually paddled to the left, which brought her in the opposite direction of downtown, but this morning she decided to change it up and glided along the water toward her shop. Hmmm, maybe she should make this her new method of commuting. It was certainly more enjoyable than sitting in the Boston traffic she had fought for so many years. Connie wondered for a moment how Ginger would take to riding to *Just Jewelry* on a paddleboard but quickly dismissed the idea. A wet dog with sand clinging to her belly would not be good for the cleanliness of her shop.

Between the rhythm of her paddling and the occasional seagull or two gliding past her, Connie's excursion had just the effect she had been hoping for. All thoughts of Allister's murder disappeared from her mind, and instead her heart filled with gratitude for the blessings that surrounded her.

That is, until the pier came into view in the distance.

She had always admired the weather-beaten wooden structure towering above the Gulf and jetting out towards the horizon. Was she now forever destined to associate that pier with tragedy?

Giving her shoulders a reprieve from the paddling motion, Connie sat on the paddleboard and tucked her legs beneath her. As the board floated up and down with the waves, she let them carry her slowly towards the shore, while her gaze remained fixed on the pier. "If only you could talk. What would you tell me?" she whispered.

Of her four suspects - Paige, Abby, Isabel, and Mary Ann - none of them seemed like a killer. But then again, it wasn't like murderers were known to act in any specific way. Otherwise, they would be easy to catch.

With the second session of her two-part class due to take place in five days, Connie was anxious to have the mystery solved. At this rate, the only students left would be Gertrude and Emma.

The sun was getting stronger, so Connie jumped off her board and dunked under the water. Then she rested her arms on the board and let the waves gently rock her, as if she were in a cradle.

Usually the ocean water back home in New England was still quite cold in late June, but here the water temperature had already climbed into the mid-eighties. Despite its warmth, it still cooled her off. Connie felt sufficiently refreshed to paddle home.

She arrived in the shop a little after 9:00, and Grace was thrilled that she took the time for a paddle. "I saw you head out with your paddleboard this morning while I was having coffee on my balcony, so I came in a little early, just in case."

"What would I do without you?" Connie asked.

"I hope you never have to find out."

Connie wholeheartedly agreed.

In between the occasional customer, Connie and Grace chatted the morning away, discussing everything from the latest news on their own families to Emma's struggles accepting the changes in her family life. Although they were technically working, it felt more like a day off than a workday. Despite everything, life was good.

As the morning turned into early afternoon, the conversation inevitably turned toward lunch.

I'm tired of sandwiches," Connie said. "How does an entree from *Gallagher's* sound? My treat."

Grace nodded in agreement. "Sounds wonderful."

Connie pulled out a menu she had stored behind the checkout desk and decided on a southwest chicken and rice bowl. "Gallagher's bowls are huge. This ought to hold me over until I get home tonight."

Since Grace would be leaving in a couple of hours, she opted for a chicken Caesar salad.

Grace called in the order while Connie fastened Ginger's leash. Then she threw her pocketbook over her shoulder, which seemed to be getting heavier by the day. *I've got to empty this thing out, or I'm going to injure myself,* she thought.

"I'll be back in about a half hour. I'm going to take Ginger for a walk before picking up our lunches," Connie called out as she exited through the back door.

Since Grace was minding the store, it was nice not to have to worry about staying within view of the front door. Connie and Ginger strolled through the streets that ran adjacent to the beach, then headed in the direction of the pier. It was so hot that if felt like she was walking through an oven. Connie thought about turning back, but she resisted the urge, since Ginger needed the exercise.

When they reached the short street that led to the pier, Connie allowed Ginger to pull her toward *Friendly Scoops,* where the dog apparently remembered that Emily kept a bowl of water for four-legged passersby. Seeing Ginger take a drink reminded Connie that she was beginning to get thirsty, as well. Since she hadn't thought to bring a bottle of water, she went inside to buy one. She looked around for Emily but, not seeing her, she took her water to a bench in the shade facing the pier to breathe in the fresh air. She still had a few minutes left before her order at *Gallagher's* would be ready.

While Connie was relaxing, she caught sight of an energetic little boy admiring Ginger from a bench a short distance away. He asked his mother if he could go pet the dog, but the mother was too busy trying to pacify a crying infant to bring him over. "When I get your brother to stop crying, if the dog is still there, we'll go say hi."

Seeing the disappointment on the child's face, Connie brought Ginger over to them, leaving her cumbersome purse on her own bench, since it wasn't too far away. "Hi, I'm Connie, and this is Ginger. She's very friendly."

The woman gave Connie a grateful smile as the boy sat on the ground to play with the dog. Ginger, of course, basked in the attention.

"I'm Tammy, and the dog lover here is my son Jacob. And this noisy little guy is Jack."

Jack finally stopped crying, so Tammy put him back in his stroller.

"Mom, can we get a dog like Ginger?" Jacob asked.

But Connie could tell from the exhausted look on Tammy's face that that wasn't happening anytime in the near future.

"How about we talk about it when you get a little older?"

He looked up at Connie and sulked. "That means no."

After chatting for a few minutes, Connie excused herself. She went back to her bench and pulled her phone from her purse to check the time. It had been about a half hour since Grace called in the food order, so it should be about ready. As she slipped the phone back in her purse, she noticed a folded sheet of paper that she didn't remember seeing before, resting on top of her wallet. The paper was clean and unwrinkled, as if someone had just placed it there.

What on earth is this? she asked herself, unfolding the typewritten note. She held in her hand what appeared to be a limerick. Confused, she read the poem:

A jewelry maker in Sapphire Beach,

Has a desire to teach.
If she seeks to expose,
She should stay on her toes,
Or like Allister, she'll be dead on the beach.

Connie could practically hear the blood pumping through her veins as she looked around for any clue as to who could have left the strange, but clear, note. But there was nobody in the vicinity who looked familiar or suspicious. She took a few steps and scanned the boulevard in both directions. Still nobody.

The family she and Ginger had visited with earlier was still at the same bench. Connie asked Tammy if she had seen anything, but she hadn't. Of course, how could she have with two young children to keep an eye on?

After searching for a few more minutes, Connie took a picture of the note and texted it to Josh and Zach, then left.

Within seconds, Josh had responded: *Zach's working on another case, but I'm on my way to* Just Jewelry.

Connie immediately returned to the store. She didn't want to worry Grace, but she had no choice but to show her the note. With Josh on his way, she couldn't hide it.

After Connie did her best to relay what happened, Grace snatched the note from her hand to examine it. She shook her head. "I don't like this one bit. This means that the killer was following you this afternoon."

Connie didn't want to mention it, but she couldn't help but notice that the killer had waited until she was near the pier to make his or her statement. That couldn't be a coincidence.

"Tell me everything you did today, Connie," Josh said, as soon as he arrived. "Don't leave out anything."

Connie did her best to recount the events of what, until a few minutes ago, she had considered an uneventful day.

"I don't like this at all," Grace said. "Who knows how long this person has been watching you?"

"I have to agree," Josh said. "You need to be extra vigilant until we catch this person."

"It seems clear that the killer is from Florida Sands," Grace said. "Why else would they have sent you a limerick?"

"And a bad limerick at that!" Connie said. "I was thinking about that, too. Maybe the person wanted me to think it was someone from the English Department. Being a professor and English majors, it seems that if it was Isabel, Paige, or Abby, they could have written something a little more eloquent."

Josh chuckled. "I'm sure the person didn't spend a lot of time polishing their work. They weren't trying to win a literary award; they were just trying to send you a clear message."

"Unfortunately, they succeeded," Grace said.

Josh pointed toward Connie's laptop. "I'll need to check out whatever surveillance footage you have. Why don't I take a quick look now?"

They each pulled up a chair around the table, and Connie opened the security software. Josh fast forwarded through the day, but nothing looked out of the ordinary.

Josh asked Connie to send him the video file, which she did on the spot. "I'll take a closer look later, but I don't think there's anything here."

Suddenly, Connie remembered mentioning to Mary Ann on Monday that she had sent the police surveillance footage of the night Allister was killed. "Do you think the person kept their distance from the store because they knew that I had security cameras? I did mention it to Mary Ann when I talked to her last Monday."

"A lot of downtown shops have cameras. Whoever did this might have just assumed that you did, as well. But I'll keep that in mind."

So would Connie.

Shortly after Josh left, taking the limerick with him, Gallagher came in with the women's lunch order. With all the activity, Connie had completely forgotten about their food.

"I saw the police car parked in front of your shop, so I figured you forgot about lunch."

After they caught Gallagher up on what had happened, he insisted that lunch was on the house. "It's the least I can do after the rough day you two have had."

Although it was long past the end of Grace's shift, at first she refused to leave Connie alone in the store.

However, after Gallagher promised to check in on Connie periodically, she finally relented.

Chapter 15

AFTER THE 7:00 MASS on Sunday morning, Connie texted Elyse. *Is Emma free today?*

Are you dumping me for Emma now?

Haha, very funny. I was wondering if you could bring her by the store for a tutoring session. I have a plan that goes beyond jewelry making.

After a few minutes, Elyse's response came: *Sounds mysterious, I love it! Emma would love to come. She is so excited. We are going to the 11:00 Mass, and I'll drop her off right after. Your timing is perfect. She could use some time away from Victoria.*

Elyse arrived just before 12:30 with two sandwiches and two bags of chips, one for Connie and one for Emma. Connie had insisted that Grace take the day off, since she worked extra hours on

Friday, thanks to the funeral mix-up, and again on Saturday because of the limerick incident.

"Thanks for lunch," Connie said, unwrapping the turkey and swiss sandwich as if she hadn't eaten in days.

"No problem. You two have fun. Josh got called into work, so Victoria and I are going for a swim. I'll be back in a couple of hours."

After eating their sandwiches, Connie cleaned off the table and pulled out some supplies, while Emma showed her what she had accomplished so far.

As they were about to get started, a customer came through the door. Connie greeted the woman, told her a little about the shop, and pointed out the Fair Trade section. "You can read about our international artisans if you would like to learn more about them," she said, pointing to the framed photos and biographies scattered throughout the section.

While the customer was browsing, Connie reminded Emma of what she had taught her last Thursday in class, then went to the register to ring up the customer, who chose a bracelet from Ecuador. Connie thanked her and returned to Emma, who was making decent progress.

About 1:00, Connie's cell phone rang, indicating that her sister was trying to reach her via FaceTime.

Gianna was right on time.

Connie had filled in her sister on Emma's struggles adjusting to having Victoria in the family and asked her to call once she put her three-year-old twins, Hannah and Noah, down for a nap.

"It's my sister, Gianna. Would you like to meet her?"

Emma nodded enthusiastically, so Connie pulled up a chair next to Emma and accepted the call.

"Hi Gi, I'm here with Emma. She'd like to meet you."

"Hi sweetie, I'm Gianna," Gi said, waving to Emma.

Emma waved back. "Hi Gianna."

"I'm teaching Emma how to make a bracelet," Connie said. Emma held up her creation for Gianna to see. "She is quite talented."

"You're learning from the best," Gianna said.

Emma smiled.

Connie said to Emma, "Gianna is not only my sister, she is one of my best friends. But it wasn't always that way, was it Gi?"

Both women laughed, and Gianna shook her head violently back and forth. "She used to torture me when we were kids."

"Yeah, sorry about that, sis. But you have to admit, it helped make you the strong, no-nonsense woman that you are today."

"Yeah, thanks for that," Gi said, sarcastically.

"I have a little sister, too. Her name is Victoria," Emma said. "She's cute but really needy. She always wants *something*. It's kind of a drag sometimes. I can never be alone with my parents, and we always have to go home early."

Gianna looked thoughtfully at Emma across the fifteen hundred miles that separated them. "I can see how that would be a drag, especially when it's thrown upon you all of a sudden."

"I don't remember this," Connie said, "but our parents tell us that I used to ask if we could send Gianna back when we were little."

Emma laughed. Then her expression grew serious. "Sometimes I feel that way, too."

"I get that it's a big change for you, honey," Connie said. "But I'm so glad we didn't send Gi back. Sometimes the best blessings in life don't feel like blessings at all in the beginning. We have to grow into the really big ones."

"Connie's right," Gianna said. "I didn't like getting bossed around as a kid, but now, I couldn't imagine my life without Connie. A sister is someone who will always be there for you to listen and share your dreams. I always looked up to Connie, and, believe me, you'll need someone to take your parents' focus off you when you get a little older."

"Hmmm, I never thought of it that way. Do you think Victoria will look up to me when we're older?"

"She already does," Connie said. "That's why she copies everything you do. Being a big sister is a huge responsibility. You have an impressionable little mind watching everything you do."

Emma appeared to consider this possibility.

"Sometimes I just need some space, though," she said. "She's literally *always* there."

"I'll tell you what," Connie said. "Whenever you need to get away, you can come to *Just Jewelry*. We can work on jewelry, or you can play with Ginger - whatever you want. And when I hire more employees, we can even go to the beach sometimes or out for ice cream. Don't be afraid to tell your

Mom when you need to get away. She'll understand."

Emma almost knocked Connie out of her seat with a hug. "Thanks, Connie."

They finished their conversation with Gianna, and Connie promised to call soon to speak with the twins.

After they hung up, Emma went back to work on her bracelet. She appeared to be thinking while she worked and a few minutes later, she suddenly looked at Connie. "Did you and Gianna plan this conversation so you could try to convince me that I should give Victoria another chance?"

Connie put both hands in the air and laughed. "Okay, you caught me, I asked Gi to call when I knew you'd be here. But it's only because I care about you, and I want you and Victoria to be as close as Gi and I are."

Emma smiled. "I'll think about it."

"Fair enough," Connie said. "That's all I ask. And I meant it. I know what it's like to need to get away from your baby sister for a little while. You are welcome here any time. We big sisters have to stick together."

Just then, a young couple walked through the door.

"Emma, do you remember what I said to the last lady who came?"

"About the Fair Trade items and the artisans?"

Connie nodded.

"Yes, I think so."

"Why don't you handle these customers then. That way, you can help me in the shop when you visit."

Emma jumped up and greeted the couple in her most professional tone. Connie stood a few yards behind Emma for moral support. To Connie's surprise, Emma gave them the spiel just as well as Connie could have, but with some added cuteness. She peeked over her shoulder for confirmation that she had done it right, and Connie nodded and winked.

When the woman bought a couple of pairs of earrings, Connie instructed Emma on how to wrap the jewelry in tissue paper and place it in a bag.

"That was fun," Emma said as the customers were leaving.

By the time Elyse returned with Victoria, Emma was running the show, with a little backup from Connie on the cash register. Her demeanor had changed, and she even gave Victoria a hug upon seeing her.

Emma told Elyse about all the things she had learned, but refused to show her the progress she had made on the bracelet. Connie and Emma had worked out a little surprise, and Emma swore Connie to secrecy.

As they left, Elyse mouthed, "Thank you."

Connie was thrilled that she could help. Who knew, maybe in a few years, she could employ young Emma.

Chapter 16

ON MONDAY MORNING, Connie arrived at *Just Jewelry*, disengaged the alarm, and tidied up the shop before flipping the sign on her front door to say "open." She was painfully aware that there were only four days left until her class would meet again, and she had been hoping their last session would feel like friends reuniting for a final visit. But the unsolved murder looming over their heads greatly diminished the warm and fuzzy feeling she hoped to engender. Under the circumstances, she wouldn't be surprised if nobody showed up.

Connie tried to remain optimistic, but she was having trouble maintaining a cheerful demeanor. When Grace's shift ended after lunch, Connie thought she was leaving for the day. But she was surprised to see her return a few minutes later with a large cup of mint chocolate chip ice cream.

"I love that you're trying to cheer me up with ice cream," Connie said. "But it's not like I just had a bad date! If word gets out that a man was murdered with my pliers, and that I have a killer in my jewelry-making class, *Just Jewelry* is toast."

Grace put an affectionate arm around Connie's shoulders. "I know ice cream doesn't solve everything," she said, "but it won't make things any worse."

It was hard to argue with that logic. Connie offered a spoon to Grace, but she refused.

"It's all for you, honey. I have some errands to run."

And with that, Grace was out the door, like an ice cream-bearing superhero.

Connie brought her ice cream and her laptop over to the table. With no solid leads on the case, she decided to do an online search for Allister McCue to see if she could come up with anything besides work that would connect him to anyone who was in her class.

It quickly became evident that Allister was a prolific academic writer. There were numerous links to articles he authored, and she even came across a few book reviews. Connie clicked on one of the reviews and was brought to a blog. It seems Allister had a personal blog where he reviewed books.

She scanned through several of them and quickly discovered that Allister wasn't afraid to tear books, or authors, apart. It crossed Connie's mind that someone may have killed him over a terrible review. If he broke someone's career, that could be motive for murder. But since the killer had to have had access to Connie's pliers, and nothing pointed to anyone in the class, she dismissed that idea and moved on.

She also came across his biography on the university's website, which noted he was a member of the Admissions Committee. Didn't Paige say that Mary Ann's son was denied admission to Florida Sands? If Allister was to blame, that might explain the hatred that Mary Ann had for him.

The sound of the door chime pulled Connie from her thoughts. It was Isabel. She looked like she'd been through the ringer, but Connie wasn't surprised.

Allister's death certainly turned what could have been a quiet summer on campus into a trying one.

Connie closed out her internet search and greeted Isabel, then went out back to retrieve her rain jacket.

"I would have dropped this by the college," Connie said, handing her the jacket. "You didn't have to come all the way here."

"It's no problem at all," Isabel said. "I was actually looking for an excuse to get off campus for a little while, and I remembered that I still hadn't picked it up."

"You're just in time," Connie said. "We're supposed to get thundershowers today."

"We get thundershowers every day this time of year," she said playfully.

"Very true."

As Isabel was about to leave, Connie decided it might be her only chance to find out about Mary Ann's son.

"Isabel, I haven't been able to get Allister's untimely death off my mind. It really bothers me that he was killed with my pliers."

"I hope you don't think that anyone in the English Department blames you for what happened," she said. "There is no way you could have known that someone would steal your pliers."

Even though she knew it wasn't her fault, hearing Isabel's words still made her feel better. Connie shook her head. "It's not that. Like everyone else, I'm sure, I just want justice to be served."

"I'm sure the police will get to the bottom of it. From what I hear, they are still following up on leads."

"There's just something that's been bothering me," Connie said. "I understand that Mary Ann's son was denied admission to Florida Sands, and I understand that Allister was on the Admissions Committee."

Connie could tell by Isabel's expression that she understood the direction Connie was going in with her questions. The look of understanding on her face was replaced with one of contemplation.

"I never thought of that, Connie, but yes, it's true. Allister was influential in Ian being denied admission."

"Did Mary Ann know that?" Connie asked. "I would imagine those proceedings would be confidential."

"They should have been," Isabel said. "But one time Allister was in my office talking about how poor Ian's writing skills were and how he wasn't bright enough for Florida Sands. I defended him, saying he wasn't applying to be an English major, but Allister was being a jerk." She let out a deep breath. "He didn't realized Mary Ann was seated at her desk. We weren't positive that she heard what he said but, from that point on, her attitude toward him changed. It was as if she couldn't stand to be in the same room with him. She tried to hide the fact that she was disappointed he got tenure, but it was obvious that she was hoping he would be denied and would go somewhere else."

Connie remembered how Mary Ann looked like someone had punched her in the gut while Allister was praising the high caliber of students at Florida Sands. Had she killed him in retribution?

"I'd better get going," Isabel said, folding her raincoat over her arm. "It's been a long day, and I have a lot to get done this afternoon."

When Isabel left, Connie sat on the couch, where she could people-watch through the front window.

She was pleasantly surprised to see Elyse stroll down the sidewalk and into *Just Jewelry*.

"What brings you by this time of day?" Connie asked. By late afternoon, Elyse was usually still working or with her girls.

"I just finished a showing nearby and thought I'd stop by before picking up Victoria from daycare and Emma from volleyball camp."

"In that case," Connie said, "I made some of my famous lemonade that you love so much. I'll get us a couple of glasses."

"Perfect," Elyse said, as she let herself drop onto the sofa. "I could use a pick-me-up."

Connie poured two tall glasses of her famous lemonade, which consisted of the perfect combination of watermelon and lemon juice. It was one of Connie's favorite healthy mid-afternoon drinks. She brought them out, along with some cocktail napkins, on a white tray with painted hydrangeas.

"Ooh, fancy," Elyse said. She took a long sip, then placed it on the tray, which Connie had put on top of the coffee table. "I wanted to thank you for talking to Emma on Sunday. Things aren't perfect, but I'm noticing a definite difference in her behavior towards Victoria."

It boosted Connie's confidence to know that she had helped to solve at least one problem this week. "She'll find her way. She just needs time to adjust. Emma's a good kid with a good heart."

Elyse smiled and nodded. "How are *you* doing? Are you still planning to hold the second session of your jewelry-making class on Thursday night?"

"I'm not sure who will come, but I'll be here for whoever would like to attend. I'd be surprised if anyone from Florida Sands shows up, though."

"Well, I will definitely be taking Emma and Gertrude. Emma is excited about finishing her bracelet. She won't show it to me until it's finished."

"Yes, she has a little surprise planned, but you won't get any information from me," she said, pretending to zip her mouth and throw away the key.

Elyse laughed. "I wouldn't dream of it."

"I was hoping the police would have made an arrest by now," Connie said.

"I know. Me, too. How is your investigation going?"

"Slowly," Connie said. She filled Elyse in on what Isabel said when she came by.

"So, who is your strongest suspect?" Elyse asked. "Now that we know it's not Jerry," she added with a chuckle.

Connie recounted her conversation with Isabel. "This makes Mary Ann an obvious suspect. If she was angry enough at Allister for contributing to her son being denied admission, it could be her."

"Have you crossed Abby or Paige off your list?" Elyse asked.

Connie shook her head. "Between Abby's plagiarism and Allister dating Paige's mother, they both had a motive."

"So, besides those three," Elyse said, "the only other person it could be is Isabel."

"Pretty much. According to Abby, there were signs that Allister wanted her job."

"It's not the strongest motive, but people *have* killed for less," Elyse said.

They sipped their lemonade in silence for a few minutes and gazed out the window, watching passersby, until, suddenly, dark clouds moved aggressively across the sky.

"I think that's my cue," Elyse said, placing her empty glass on the tray. "If I don't want to get drenched, I'd better leave now."

Chapter 17

ON TUESDAY MORNING, Abby called.

"I'm so sorry to have to tell you this but, given everything that happened with Dr. McCue, our group is going to discontinue the jewelry-making class. I, for one, plan to come in to finish my necklace at some point this week, but Isabel decided that, given the circumstances, it wouldn't be appropriate to complete the class."

A wave of disappointment came over Connie when she heard the news. She pretty much expected that the group would cancel, but she couldn't help but feel disheartened. Her first jewelry-making class was officially a bust.

"Thank you for the call," Connie said, trying to hide her regret. "Come by anytime to work on your necklace."

Abby promised to stop in soon.

Connie sat facing her Wall of Fame and leaned her arms against the sturdy oak table. After her grand opening, she had created a collage of framed photos of friends and loved ones, whom she considered to be part of the *Just Jewelry* family, and dubbed it the Wall of Fame. It included pictures of her Aunt Concetta, her family back in Boston, Natasha, and friends and customers in Sapphire Beach. All the people in this world and some in heaven, whom she least wanted to disappoint, seemed to be looking back at her with pity.

"I'll figure something out," she said, speaking to the group as if it were assembled in her shop. "This is *not* going ruin my dream."

She scooped up Ginger, who apparently came to the front of the shop to see who she was talking to, and placed her on her lap. As she stroked the silky fur on top of Ginger's head, she tried to look on the bright side. She still had Gertrude, Emma, and Jerry. That is, if Jerry didn't cancel. But she held out hope, since he had a gift to complete for his wife. Besides, he might welcome the chance to get his mind of his brother's death.

Connie had been so lost in thought that she jumped when she heard the ringtone on her cell phone. It was her second favorite detective.

"Hi, Josh."

"Connie, I'm glad I caught you. I would like you to look at some evidence we found at the crime scene. There is something we are hoping you might be able to shed some light on."

"I'd be happy to." Anything to help get this murder solved.

"Can you come down to the station?"

"I'm sorry, but I'm alone all day in the store, and there's nobody to cover for me. If it's time sensitive, you could come here."

"Okay, I'll be there as soon as I can," he said.

About an hour later, both Josh and Zach were sitting at the table in her shop. She didn't expect to see Zach. After all, it only took one person to show her some evidence.

Before Josh had a chance to pull out the photos, Connie asked, "Can you tell me if you're close to making an arrest?" After the group from Florida Sands pulled out of her class, she was more anxious than ever to have the case solved.

"We can't discuss the details of the case, but we are still exploring leads," Zach said, still all official in his demeanor. If she wasn't mistaken, he looked nervous.

"As you can imagine, people are dropping out of my class. Is there anything you can tell me? Does anyone in the class have an alibi?" She was hoping to cross at least someone off her list.

Josh and Zach exchanged a mischievous glance. "Of the people who were in your class, I'm happy to say that Elyse, Emma, Gertrude, and Grace all went for ice cream. After that, Gertrude and Grace talked into the evening. So, they are all off the hook."

"Well, *that's* good to know," Connie said, matching their sarcasm. "I was afraid that Gertrude and Emma were a dangerous duo."

Zach shot her an amused look.

"You guys know what I mean," Connie said, happy to see they had both relaxed.

"We can tell you that Jerry had a solid alibi, which you know courtesy of Gertrude's follies," Josh said.

Connie had to laugh. "That was hilarious. You should have been there when Jerry walked into what we thought was *his* wake."

"What I wouldn't give to have been a fly on the wall," Zach said, laughing.

"Anyone else?" Connie asked.

"It turns out that Paige had an alibi after all," Zach said. "The preliminary autopsy report determined that the time of death was approximately 11:00 PM. She lives in an off-campus apartment, and when we originally tried to check her alibi, nobody could verify that she was at home. But her next-door neighbor, another student who had been out of town for the night when we initially tried to reach her, was able to vouch for Paige. She saw hers return home at 10:00, and she said Paige's car was still in her parking spot when she went to bed after midnight. Of the four from Florida Sands, Paige is the only one with an alibi."

Connie was glad to hear that. Paige was a kind young woman with a promising future, and she was happy to know she wasn't the killer. "So that leaves Abby, Mary Ann, and Isabel," Connie said.

"Unless somebody else somehow managed to get their hands on your pliers. But we know for sure from your security camera footage that nobody entered the store after you left," Zach said.

"If the killer was not in your class, he or she would have to have stolen the pliers from someone who was in the class," Josh said.

"I suppose that's another possible scenario," Connie said.

"There were about two hours between the end of class and the time of Allister's death," Zach said. "It's unlikely, but it's not impossible."

"So, you had some evidence you wanted me to take a look at?" Connie asked.

"Yes," Josh said, placing a plastic bag containing six orange beads on the table in front of Connie. "We found these six beads in the sand next to Allister's body. Do you recognize them?"

Connie examined them closely to be sure, but she immediately knew where they came from. "These are the beads we used in class. But you should know that Paige, Abby, and Isabel were the only three who elected to make orange necklaces. The other three, besides Emma who was making a bracelet, made the same necklace but with turquoise beads."

"What color beads was Allister working with?"

"Turquoise."

"So, these beads had to have come from Paige, Abby, or Isabel?" Josh asked, apparently wanting to be certain he understood correctly.

"That's correct."

And since Paige's alibi was verified, that meant that the killer had to be Abby or Isabel.

Connie felt a surge of excitement knowing they were closing in on the killer.

"Thank you, Connie. That helps a lot," Josh said.

After they both stood up to leave, Josh caught Zach's attention and gestured toward Connie.

Zach hesitated, but after a moment, he nodded.

"I'll meet you outside. I think you two have something to talk to about," Josh said, leaving Connie and Zach alone together in the store.

Chapter 18

A COUPLE OF TIMES, Zach opened his mouth to say something, but before anything coherent came out, he closed it again.

After all the mixed signals he had been sending over the past couple of months, it was really up to Zach to start the conversation, but since the guy looked like he was in agony, Connie took pity and did what she could to help him along.

Connie motioned for Zach to take a seat on an armchair, and she sat on the couch facing him. It was better than standing awkwardly in the middle of the store.

"Whatever it is you want to say, it's okay," Connie said. "I enjoyed our date in March, but it's okay with me if you only want to be friends." Since they shared a few close mutual friends in Sapphire Beach, Connie didn't want either of them to be uncomfortable when they were all together.

Zach's expression was a cross between frustration and concern.

"No, Connie, please don't think that. I very much enjoyed our date, too. I truly respect you, and I'm so glad you came into my life."

Connie gave him a confused look, and Zach shifted in his seat.

"I'm not saying this right," he said. "What I mean is I *do* want to take you out again. But I'm not sure if it's a good idea."

Connie wondered if it was because she had ended up in the middle of his last three murder investigations. Was it becoming too difficult to separate his work life from his personal life? "Why wouldn't it be a good idea?" she asked.

Finally, Zach seemed to regain his confidence and looked squarely at Connie. "I was offered a job at a department back home, and I'm considering taking it. I really do want to take you out again, but I'm afraid it would be too difficult to continue seeing each other when my future is so uncertain."

Now it was Connie's turn to become tongue-tied. She couldn't decide if that was good news or bad news. On one hand, she was glad that Zach's feelings for her hadn't changed, but on the other hand, there was a real possibility that he may walk out of her life forever.

"I love it here in Sapphire Beach," he continued, "but my brother's kids are growing up fast. I got a call from a sergeant in the police department in the town where my brother lives, which is just outside of Chicago. It's the same town we grew up in, and my parents are still there, as well. It's a good offer, and I'd be crazy not to consider it." He paused and then added, "But just for the record, if I do take it, one of my biggest regrets would be that you and I never got a chance."

Connie managed a half smile. "It seems like the odds are stacked against us. When we met, I was planning to return to Boston, and now that I am settled in Sapphire Beach, you may be leaving."

He nodded and stared at the floor for a moment.

"But you have to do what will make you happiest, Zach," Connie said. "It would be pretty amazing to be a detective in your hometown, if that's where you want to be. I understand your dilemma and promise to keep your decision in prayer."

"Thank you for not making this harder than it needs to be," he said, embracing her gently as she stood to walk him to the door. "I will let you know as soon as I make a decision. I haven't been able to concentrate on much else since receiving the job offer, and I have a feeling that won't change until I figure this out."

After Zach left, Connie decided she needed to get out and clear her head. Since she couldn't go far, she took Ginger for a brief walk, staying within sight of *Just Jewelry*. When she returned, she continued working on her necklace. But she couldn't stop her mind from wandering.

Connie told herself that, since all she could do was wait for Zach to make his decision, it was pointless to dwell on it. What would be, would be, right? But still, it was hard to put it out of her mind. Of course, Connie hoped Zach wouldn't take the job in Illinois, but she also knew how hard it was to leave family behind, especially the little ones. If Zach wasn't completely sure he wanted to remain in Sapphire Beach, she'd rather know now than down the line, when she might be more invested in their relationship.

Connie thought back on their brief time together. Her gaze drifted toward a painting hanging on the driftwood accent wall of a parasailer floating above the Gulf of Mexico that he had offered her as a gift when he thought she was returning to Boston permanently. Zach had wanted to give her something that would remind her of Sapphire Beach, and she had been so touched by his gesture that she gave the beautiful painting a prime spot in her store.

They only had one date, and it had certainly been one for the books, but, as she thought about it, she realized that Zach had been present at every significant moment of her life in Sapphire Beach. He was there when she announced to her friends that she would open *Just Jewelry* and relocate to Sapphire Beach. He sent her postcards while she was back in Boston for six weeks transitioning out of her job and wrapping up her affairs in Boston. And then there was that unforgettable parasailing date, after which they had both expressed a desire to see one another again. And how could she forget his support and presence at the grand opening of her store? He was even on her Wall of Fame. So much life had been packed into the last five months that she felt like she had known Zach forever.

Connie let out a frustrated sigh. It wasn't as easy as she thought it would be to put the whole thing out of her mind. So, she tried a different tactic and focused her attention on the orange beads that were found in the sand next to Allister's body.

There was no way those beads could have been at the crime scene unless they were brought there by Paige, Abby, or Isabel. And Paige had an alibi, so Connie was down to two suspects. For the first time in nearly two weeks, she felt a glimmer of hope that the crime might soon be solved. She couldn't interfere with the investigation by confronting Abby and Isabel, but, with a little luck, the police would find their answers and soon make an arrest.

Customers trickled in and out of the store throughout the day, mostly buying less expensive items, such as a pair of earrings or an inexpensive bracelet.

About 5:00, Connie sipped on some iced tea while she watched the crowd with their umbrellas and tents in tow make their way off the beach. She watched two women drop off their gear in an SUV, then proceed to do some window shopping. They eventually made their way into *Just Jewelry*.

"It looks like it's about to downpour," Connie said, after greeting the women, whose cheeks were pink from a day in the sun. Gray clouds were slowly beginning to make their presence felt.

"I think you're right, but we saw your display window on our way to the beach earlier, and we just had to come in," one of the women said. "I'm Joyce, and this is Alice."

"It's a pleasure to meet you both. I'm Connie."

Joyce picked up multi-strand necklace made of mixed-sized red coral beads that Connie had finished a few weeks before. "You have some beautiful pieces."

"Thank you," Connie said. "I recently finished that piece. The beads are Mediterranean coral." It had taken Connie more than forty hours of tedious work to create it. She had hesitated to purchase the expensive beads but had fallen in love with them. The price of the necklace reflected both the premium cost of the beads and her many hours of disciplined work. The profit from that piece alone could pay Grace's salary for a month.

Connie called to their attention the matching earrings and bracelet, which she had displayed next to the necklace.

"Oooh, these are exquisite," Alice said. "Do you know who would love these?"

Both women said in unison, "Diane."

Joyce explained to Connie that Diane was a mutual friend who was feeling down, because her youngest daughter would be going off to college in California next month. It was their friend's birthday the following weekend, and the three women had dinner plans on Friday to celebrate.

"These would be just the gift to cheer her up," Alice said, holding the matching bracelet and earrings next to the necklace. "How about if we split the cost and give it to her as a birthday gift?"

Joyce happily agreed, and Connie rang up the matching pieces, splitting the payment equally between each woman's credit card. It was the largest sale Connie had made in the three months she had been in business.

When Joyce and Alice left, Connie felt as though she was walking on air. She had needed something positive to happen after the Florida Sands group dropped out of her class and receiving Zach's news.

With newfound motivation, Connie designed a poster that she had been meaning to make to let customers know that she offered custom jewelry for bridal parties. She tweaked the text and the images until she was satisfied, then printed the 8 ½ by 11-inch flyer, mounted it in a gold frame, and strategically placed it on the checkout counter.

She glanced at her phone to check the time. The evening was still young, so, with new energy, she decided to complete the necklace she had been working on.

But first it would be a good time to call her parents.

Chapter 19

CONNIE MADE IT A POINT to call her parents at
least once a week, and this time of day they were
most likely unwinding before dinner. Connie's
father, Greg, was an accountant who ran his own
firm, and her mother, Josephine, along with Gianna,
owned a home staging company together.

Right after the first ring, her mother's soothing
voice melted away the fifteen hundred miles that
separated them. "Hi, sweetie, good timing. Dinner is
in the oven, and your dad and I were just relaxing."
Connie smiled at their comforting predictability.
"Are you hanging in there?"

She had already told her about what happened
with Allister, so she guessed that that was what her
mother was referring to.

"Yeah. The police haven't yet made an arrest, but I'm doing okay. Although I'm still a little concerned about how this might affect enrollment in my future classes."

"Dad says to be careful and make sure you set the alarm whenever you leave the store. With all these murders lately in Sapphire Beach, your father and I feel better knowing Zach is watching out for you."

Connie decided not to mention her earlier conversation with Zach. She didn't feel like talking about it, since there was nothing she could do to change the situation. If it became necessary, she would tell them about it when Zach made his final decision.

"Both Zach and Josh are working hard to solve this case," Connie said. "But on a more positive note, I just made my biggest sale yet." Connie told her mom about the pieces she sold and how the women were buying them for a friend who was feeling low. "Not only was it great for business, but I love knowing that my creations might bring someone joy during a difficult time."

Jo squealed and related the news to Greg. "That's wonderful, honey. We're so proud of you."

"Way to go," her father said, briefly taking the phone from her mother. "It will be the first of many, I'm sure."

Connie could hear the microwave timer go off in the background. "Sounds like dinner's ready. I'll let you go."

"Yup, that's the timer for our chicken. But before I hang up, your dad and I were wondering if you plan to come home for a visit anytime soon."

Connie let out a deep breath. "I really wish I could, Mom, but it's just Grace and me in the store, and she's only part time. I do plan on hiring additional help in the fall, but I don't think I'll be at the point where I can leave things until probably next year." She hated to disappoint her parents, but what could she do?

Then she added, "Actually, I've been thinking about the holidays. Why don't you, Dad, Gianna, Gary, and the twins come here for Christmas? You could see the store and get away from the cold for a little while. Then maybe next summer I will be in a place where I can come home."

Her mother hesitated. "I don't know, honey. I would love to, but you'd have to talk to your sister. I don't know how she and Gary will feel about being away from home for Christmas with the twins so young."

"I was planning to call her," Connie said. "I just wanted to get your take on it first."

"If they agree, your father and I are game."

With a glimmer of hope, Connie called Gianna as soon as she hung up with her mother and left a message on her cell phone. Then she went back to work on the necklace.

A few minutes later, she received a text from her sister: *Sorry, can't talk right now. The kids are on a sugar high. But I heard your message. I promise we'll think about coming for Christmas.*

A surge of adrenaline ran through Connie that further fueled her work on the necklace.

Within a couple of hours, it was finally complete. Connie relished the feeling of accomplishment that always came over her upon completing a piece of jewelry. One of the many things she loved about her work was that in the end, she could hold and admire the fruit of her labor. This necklace, along with the matching earrings she had completed and the bracelet she would soon get started on, would be an exquisite set.

While Connie was in the storage room tucking safely away the newly completed necklace, the door chimed. She returned to the front of the store to find Paige glancing around, presumably searching for Connie.

"Hi Paige. What a pleasant surprise. What brings you here so late?" It was nearly closing time, so Connie doubted Paige came to work on her necklace.

Paige looked relieved to have found Connie. "I'm glad I caught you here. I was at home tonight working on my necklace and, as I got to the end, I noticed that I'm missing some beads."

She pulled out her orange necklace to show Connie, then a small plastic bag containing fewer beads than would be necessary to complete her work. "I didn't notice that they were missing the last time I was here, but now that I'm almost finished, it seems clear that I'm short."

Connie took the necklace into her hands to examine it. Paige was correct. She would need several more beads to finish the project.

"That's no problem, I have some extras." Connie went over to the dentistry cabinet by the oak table where she stored many of her supplies and pulled out the beads that Paige would need. As she slipped the beads into a small plastic bag, something suddenly occurred to her. Paige's missing beads could be the ones that the police found in the sand next to Allister's body.

But Paige couldn't be the killer. Josh had verified her alibi.

Connie handed Paige the extra beads. "There should be plenty here to finish the necklace."

Paige breathed a sigh of relief. "Thanks, Connie. I was afraid that after all that work, I wouldn't be able to complete it, and I wanted to wear it on a dinner date this weekend, with a navy-blue dress I bought."

"That will look amazing," Connie said, making Paige promise to send a picture.

"Paige, can you sit down for a minute?" Connie asked, gesturing toward the oak table.

"Sure, what's up?"

"I want you to think really hard on this. Do you have any idea where you lost those orange beads?" Connie asked.

Paige shrugged her shoulders. "It could have been anywhere. Why is it so important?"

Connie wasn't sure if she should confide in Paige that the police found three orange beads at the crime scene, but there was no way around it if she wanted Paige's help. So she explained the situation.

Paige leaned forward and placed her elbows on the table. "You mean the killer stole them from me? That doesn't make any sense."

"Think hard. Were you with Abby or Isabel after class? Even briefly?"

Paige firmly shook her head back and forth. "No."

Then Connie remembered that Paige and Allister had dinner together at *Gallagher's*. "Paige, did you take out your necklace at any point during dinner to show Allister?"

She started to shake her head again, then stopped abruptly. "Wait a minute. Not in the restaurant, but do you remember how I told you that Jerry followed us out?"

"Yes."

"Well, we stopped to talk with him for a minute. He was in a sour mood, but we spoke briefly about class, and I told Jerry that I thought it was sweet that he was making an anniversary present for his wife. Allister was laying on the charm with me, still trying to get me to like him, so he told Jerry what a talented jewelry maker he thought I was, and insisted I show him my necklace. Just to humor him and because Jerry clearly wanted to get out of there, I quickly showed it to him. Then I got in my car and drove away." Paige became more animated. "When I pulled away, Allister was bending down to pick something up. I probably lost the beads when I took out my necklace in my rush to show Jerry."

"I'll bet Allister picked them up and put them in his pocket, and they fell out when he was killed. That's probably how they ended up at the crime scene."

"So Allister picked up my beads so he could return them to me. I guess that was nice of him."

"I know you didn't want Allister dating your mom - and I totally get that - but I think he really did think highly of you."

"Well, at least he cared enough to pick up my beads."

Connie put a sisterly arm around Paige's shoulders and walked her to the door. "You should go to the police station in the morning and tell Detective Josh Miller what you told me. He's the lead detective on the case. His shift starts at 9:00."

"I will," Paige said and left the store.

Now that Connie knew that the beads at the murder scene came from Paige's necklace and not the killer's Mary Ann was back on the suspect list.

***

On Wednesday morning before heading into the shop, Connie went for a quick paddle to clear her head. As she glided along the coastline, she worked on a game plan for the next couple of days. She was disappointed that the folks from Florida Sands wouldn't be present the following evening for part two of her class, but she was determined to stay positive. Business was good, especially for the slow summer months, and the police were still following up on leads.

For now, Connie was determined to devote her energies to marketing her store and helping the students she still had - Emma Gertrude, and hopefully Jerry - to complete their projects. She would finish this class strong by giving her remaining students her best effort, and once the police caught the killer, she would move forward and schedule more classes. By the time she loaded her paddleboard onto the dolly to drag it home, she felt like a new woman. She had managed to push all thoughts of killers and murder investigations out of her head. This class would be a practice run. If she could make this one succeed, the sky would be the limit.

That is, unless it crushed her.

Connie and Grace arrived in the store about the same time, and, still energized from her sale the previous day, Connie promptly got to work on the matching bracelet to the necklace and earrings she had completed, while Grace handled the occasional customer.

After lunch, Grace left and Connie spent some time posting on her social media pages and uploading new pictures onto her website, then went back to work on the bracelet. She was so engrossed in her work that, despite the door chime, she didn't see Abby until she had already entered the shop.

Chapter 20

SINCE ABBY WAS one of the three remaining suspects, Connie would rather not have been alone with her, but since it was daylight and customers were wandering in and out of the store, even if Abby was the killer, Connie felt fairly safe.

"Abby," Connie said, standing to greet the young woman. "I'm so glad you came by." At least she was glad as long as Abby wasn't the killer. "To what do I owe this pleasure?"

Abby held up her necklace. "I still want to finish this, even if our group isn't coming back tomorrow," she said.

Connie smiled and gestured to a chair at the table. "Have a seat while I get us some iced tea."

Abby thanked her, and Connie returned with two glasses, complete with fresh mint.

"I haven't made much progress on the necklace," Abby said. "Every time I start to work on it in my dorm room, I get distracted by something, so I thought I'd have a better chance of completing it here."

Connie showed Abby the piece she was working on. "Wow, I would love to be able to make something like that one day," she said, admiring the sapphire-blue bracelet-in-progress.

"It just takes practice. If you keep at it, you'll be there in no time."

The two worked in silence for a while before taking a break.

Abby seemed much more upbeat than she had the last couple of times Connie saw her. She wondered what brought about the change. "I hope you don't mind my saying it, Abby, but you seem so much happier than the last time I saw you."

Abby leaned back in her chair and smiled. "Actually, I am. I had a long talk with Dr. Spenser this morning and came clean about the whole plagiarism thing."

"Wow, you did? What happened?"

"I told her everything and showed her the paper that Dr. McCue had marked up. She believed me that it was just a careless mistake, and she said she could tell that I didn't do it on purpose. She was really cool about it. She said that Dr. McCue could be a bit harsh with those things and just told me to rewrite the paper and all would be forgotten." Abby's shoulders relaxed, as if the burden was being lifted anew by telling Connie the story. "Even though I knew it was an honest mistake, I just didn't feel right about not telling her the truth. It was as if I was profiting from Dr. McCue's death, and I didn't want that on my conscience for the rest of my life."

It seemed Abby really was a good person. After learning about the health challenges that she had overcome as a teenager, Connie would have hated to see her throw it all away. "I'm proud of you, Abby. That took a lot of courage. If Dr. Spenser had turned you in, it could have cost you your childhood dream."

Upon hearing Abby's news, Connie happily crossed her off her list of suspects. Abby's motive for killing Allister was the fact that he could ruin her future career by putting a blemish on her record. If Abby had indeed killed Allister to protect her dream, there was no way she would have confessed her plagiarism to Isabel. This left her without a motive.

Abby smiled appreciatively. "I wouldn't want my future success to be based on a lie. Now if only the police could find Dr. McCue's killer, we could put this whole nightmare behind us once and for all. Do you know if they have made any progress?" Abby asked.

"I talked to the detectives yesterday. They are still working on it."

"I keep going over everything in my mind, trying to think of anything that could shed light on who might have wanted to kill Dr. McCue, both at your class and in the English Department," Abby said.

"Did you come up with anything?"

"Not really. I was working when the police came to search his office, but they obviously didn't find anything, or they would have arrested someone by now."

"Sounds logical," Connie said. "Has the English Department started a search yet to replace him?"

"They posted the job opening this week. Dr. Spenser and a couple of other professors will be taking over his classes in the fall if they don't find anyone by then. But hopefully they will, so things can return to normal as quickly as possible."

Connie thought for a moment. "Does that mean that nobody has moved into his office yet?"

"Not yet," Abby said. "Dr. McCue's sister is coming Friday to collect his personal belongings. I assume it will get reassigned to his successor when he or she is hired."

"So, the office is exactly the way Allister left it?" Connie asked.

Abby shrugged. "I guess."

"What I wouldn't give to take a look inside. Who knows, maybe there's a clue in there."

Abby narrowed her eyes in contemplation.

"You have the strangest expression on your face," Connie said. "What are you thinking?"

"It's just, if you really wanted to take a look, I have a key. The building is always open, because there are study rooms scattered throughout. I have a key to the English Department suite, and inside the student worker's desk there is a master key that would open Dr. McCue's office."

"Don't the campus police patrol the area?"

"If anyone sees us, I could just say I forgot something in my desk. Nobody would question my being there."

Connie was excited at the prospect of getting into Allister's office. "*Just Jewelry* closes at 9:00. Can we go then?"

"I don't see why not."

"Perfect."

Both women continued working on their jewelry pieces until 9:00, then they hopped into Abby's blue Toyota and headed over to campus. They parked in a nearby lot and took the stairs up to the third floor of Alumni Hall. The student workers' desk was just around the corner from Allister's office.

Abby quickly found the key in the desk drawer and handed it to Connie. "You go ahead. I'll keep watch in case anybody wanders in."

Connie entered Allister's office and systematically examined everything. It was a small office with a desk, two burgundy armchairs facing the desk, which Connie guessed were for meetings with students, and a small wall of bookshelves. She perused the books, which were mostly literary classics and New York Times bestsellers, as well as books on the craft of writing. So far, there didn't appear to be anything unusual for an English professor's office.

Next, Connie moved on to the desk. The desktop only contained a lamp and some plastic organization trays, so Connie guessed that Allister's work projects had been reassigned to another professor.

She opened the small, thin drawer that ran across the top of the desk. Nothing but office supplies. Then she turned her attention to the remaining two drawers, located on the righthand side of the desk. Nothing out of the ordinary in the top drawer – only folders containing articles that Allister had written.

The bottom drawer was a bit of a struggle to get into, but after a little tugging, Connie was finally able to yank it open. To her disappointment, there was nothing but a drawer full of paperback novels. Her late-night trek over to Florida Sands turned out to be a waste of time. She was about to push the drawer shut when she noticed the title of one of the books on the top of the pile: *A Professor's Fantasy.*

Why did that sound familiar? She searched her memory, and just as she was about to give up, Connie remembered that it was the book that Zach and Josh were joking about at her Fourth of July get-together. She perused the books that filled the deep drawer. It seemed Allister did have a penchant for trashy novels.

Connie was debating whether she should tell Abby. It probably had nothing to do with the case, and she didn't want to ruin Abby's image of Allister as a strait-laced, learned professor who only read the highest quality literature.

But before she could make up her mind, Abby was standing in the doorway.

"What's taking so long? Did you find anything?"

Connie hesitantly held up the book. "Apparently, despite your professor's public admonition of trashy novels, he had a secret passion for them."

Abby's eyes grew wide as she practically lept over to Connie and grabbed the book.

The two women seated themselves in the armchairs, and Connie watched Abby as she perused the book.

When Abby regained her ability to speak, she said, "This is crazy! I can't believe Dr. McCue would have a pile of these books in his desk."

"Maybe there's a logical explanation," Connie said.

"Like what?"

Connie shrugged and laughed. "I have no idea."

Connie retrieved a few more books from Allister's desk so they could take a broader look at his reading preferences. "These are all written by the same author: Bella Anne Spense."

Connie flipped through each of the books to see if there were any more clues as to why Allister would be harboring these unlikely novels. Besides having the same author, each book took place in a university setting. A small university in south Florida.

As Connie looked through the final book, a photocopy of a handwritten note to the author, which had been folded and stuffed between the pages, fell onto her lap. She scanned its content, then read the most relevant portion to Abby.

This is your final chance. The next time you hear from me, it will be through my attorney. I expect to receive half of your royalties every year. Since you obviously used me as the inspiration for your main character in this series, I'm only asking for what is due me.

The letter was followed by an estimate, outlining exactly what that meant annually.

"This is definitely Dr. McCue's handwriting," Abby said. "He's written enough comments on my papers over the years for me to recognize it."

"Wow," Connie said. "Allister was blackmailing someone for a small fortune."

Abby glanced down at a book she had placed on her lap. "If Allister really was the inspiration for the main character in these books, he was more of a playboy than I realized. No wonder Paige didn't want him anywhere near her mother."

"We should get out of here," Connie said. "We've been in here for a while."

"Let's put these books back in Dr. McCue's desk and get out of this office," Abby said. "We can download an electronic copy of the books from an online retailer and study them more carefully at my desk."

Connie stuffed Allister's blackmail letter into her pocket, while Abby locked up the office and returned the key to the student workers' desk.

Then Abby sat at the desk and pulled her e-reader from her backpack, while Connie dragged over a chair. It took Abby less than a minute to download a copy of one of the books they had seen in Allister's drawer. "Judging from the price of the book, it looks like Bella Anne Spense is an indie author." Then, after glancing at the product description page, she added, "And judging from the book's ranking, she does quite well."

Abby opened the book on her e-reader.

"Bella Anne Spense," Connie said. "Why does that name sound familiar?"

Abby moved through the copyright and dedication pages of the book, taking the time to scan each page. When she came to the dedication, she read it aloud to Connie: "To all the underpaid professors. This one's for you."

Connie doubted that Bella Anne Spense would have written that if she knew she would be blackmailed by one of those underpaid professors.

Connie stood up while Abby was intently examining the book, and paced the floor next to Abby's desk, thinking aloud. "So, Allister didn't have copies of those novels, because he enjoyed reading them. He believed he was the inspiration for the main character."

"Sounds that way," Abby said, paying more attention to the book on her e-reader than to Connie.

Connie continued to pace. She found it easier to think when her body was in motion. She walked past Abby, continued beyond Allister's office, and turned around at Isabel's door, then repeated the same path a few times before pausing in front of Abby's desk. Connie leaned against the desk with her back to Abby. She scanned the room until her eyes settled on the nameplate fastened to the wall next to Isabel's door.

She stared at it for a moment, then she pressed her palm against her forehead. "Oh my goodness. Could it be?"

Abby looked up from the book. "What are you talking about?"

Connie pointed at the nameplate on Isabel's door. "Isabel Spenser. Bella Anne Spense. The names are eerily similar. What if Bella Anne Spense is a pen name for Isabel Spenser? What if they are the same person?"

Abby grew pale. "Dr. Spenser's middle name *is* Anne."

Connie jumped up from the desk, as if it burnt her. "I think we just solved the mystery. Allister wasn't interested in trashy novels. He figured out that his boss, the chair of his beloved English Department, was secretly an indie author of what he deemed to be 'trashy novels.' When he read the books, he discovered that the main character in her series was modeled after him and his escapades around the university. Instead of outing her and humiliating himself, Allister tried to blackmail Isabel for half her royalties."

As soon as the words came out of Connie's mouth, the door to the office suite slammed shut, and Isabel came into view. She leaned against the wall next to Abby's desk, staring at the women with a menacing smirk on her face.

Chapter 21

CONNIE'S MOUTH WENT DRY as she locked gazes with Isabel.

Judging from the styrofoam takeout container she was holding, Isabel hadn't left her office for the night, as Abby thought. She just went to get dinner.

There was no point in trying to save face. They were caught red-handed.

Connie pulled the blackmail letter from her pocket and waved it at Isabel. "So, Allister was blackmailing you. He found out that you were making a small fortune writing novels based on his romantic escapades, and he wanted a piece of the action."

Isabel shook her head in disgust at the mention of Allister's name. "He was an arrogant, greedy man who got what he deserved. He insisted on receiving half my profits, but there was no way he was getting his hands on any of my money. I worked hard to build my writing business over the years. I warned him several times to back off or it wouldn't end well for him."

That explained how Isabel afforded her movie-star lifestyle – the boat, the condo in Cabo, the designer clothes. She was receiving a hefty royalty check from her books to supplement her professor's income.

"So, you stole my pliers, and lured him to the pier after class to kill him?"

"During your class, Allister told me he wanted to talk to me later that evening. I told him to meet me under the pier, where we could talk in private. I just brought the pliers along as an insurance policy. I truly hoped that I wouldn't have to use them, but, as usual, Allister was uncooperative. I did my best to reason with him, but he was a stubborn fool. So, in the end, he died as he lived: an arrogant jerk."

A sinister smile crept its way onto Isabel's lips. "I guess you could call it poetic justice for the poetry professor."

Abby was unable to hide how disturbed she was by Isabel's confession.

Isabel glanced at Abby with an almost sympathetic look on her face. "You have to believe me. If there was another way to get rid of him, I would have taken it. But now that he had tenure, I couldn't exactly fire him. You know how obstinate he could be."

Isabel's eyes fell to the letter that was still in Connie's hand. "Of course, without that letter, you can't prove anything."

Isabel lunged at Connie, who side-stepped, then pushed her to the floor. She wished she had done more martial arts training lately than just hitting the heavy bag, but at least her sparring instincts were still intact.

It turned out to be just enough.

Before Isabel could get up, Connie passed the letter to Abby, who shoved it into her pocket and bolted toward the nearest stairwell. Connie ran out of the suite, slamming the door behind her, and took off behind Abby.

But she only had a few seconds' head start on Isabel. Connie looked around for anyone she could call to for help, but the academic building was nearly deserted that time of year.

The three women raced down the six flights of stairs and then down the cement stairs leading out of Alumni Hall.

"To the parking lot," Connie yelled, pointing to where Abby had left her car. However, being the Department Chair, Isabel had a prime spot reserved just for her right in front of the building. She was in her car and following Connie and Abby before they could reach the parking lot, which was still about fifty yards away.

"This way," Abby yelled, leading Connie through a wooded area that appeared to be a shortcut.

Connie ran as fast as she could, her legs burning every step of the way after descending the stairs at break-neck speed. She managed to stay a short distance behind Abby. The two women came out of the woods and into the dark parking lot right near Abby's car, but Isabel had been waiting for them in the parking lot and was driving straight towards them. Connie wondered what she would do when she caught them. Would she run them over? Surely she couldn't get away with that. Someone would be bound to notice.

Connie and Abby managed to get into the car just as Isabel pulled up beside them. Rather than exiting her car or hitting Abby's car with her own, Isabel rolled down her window and pleaded with Abby.

"Abby, I could have turned you in for plagiarism, but I didn't, because I believed you deserved a second chance. We all make mistakes. I'm asking you to give me a second chance, as well. Just wait until the morning before you turn that letter over to the police, so I can get to Cabo."

Then Isabel turned to Connie. "He was blackmailing me. He insulted my books, but he had no problem taking the profits that they earned. The hypocrite deserved what he got."

Connie cringed as she thought of her pliers being thrust into Allister. Nobody deserved *that*.

Isabel's eyes settled on Abby. She seemed to be waiting for a response to her plea. Finally, Abby nodded, apparently agreeing to give Isabel the time she needed to escape, and Isabel peeled out into the dark night.

Connie leaned back in the passenger seat of Abby's Toyota and released a deep sigh.

Turning to Abby, she said, "You know we have to go straight to the police, don't you? You don't owe Isabel anything. She killed a man."

Abby nodded. "I know. I just wanted her to leave."

A tear rolled down Abby's cheek.

It was never easy to watch a mentor fall from her pedestal. And Connie and Abby had just witnessed a monumental plummet.

While they were on their way to the police station, Connie called Josh on his cell, since it was late and she knew it was unlikely he'd still be working. He told her he'd meet them at the station and arranged to have some dispatch officers track Isabel down to bring her in for questioning. Within twenty minutes, Connie and Abby had arrived at the Sapphire Beach Police Station with Allister's blackmail letter in hand.

"Tough day at the office, huh?" Connie said jokingly to Abby as they waited in the police station waiting room to give their statements.

"I had no idea what being a student worker would entail when I applied for the job."

Chapter 22

CONNIE AND ABBY were at the police station until late Wednesday night, and by the time they finished giving their statements, Isabel was already in custody. Fortunately, the police were able to catch up with her on Route 75 at the Southwest Florida International Airport exit before she was able to make her getaway to Cabo.

First thing Thursday morning, Josh came by *Just Jewelry* to check on Connie, who was anxious to receive an update on the case.

It turned out that once they had Isabel in custody, things went a lot smoother than Connie expected they would. Knowing that the police had the copy of Allister's blackmail letter and the statements from Connie and Abby, and with some skillful interrogating on the parts of Josh and Zach, Isabel confessed to everything.

The nightmare ended just as quickly as it began.

With the killer finally behind bars, Connie decided to spend the morning making one last-ditch effort to assemble her remaining students that evening for part two of her jewelry-making class. Since many of them, including Connie, had had a grueling two weeks, she thought that finishing their projects might help everyone to move forward. So she spent the morning personally calling each student and encouraging them to return.

Connie couldn't have been more thrilled when everyone agreed to come back. Jerry was eager to finish the necklace for his wife, and the others decided that they would pay tribute to Allister by completing the class they began together.

Connie would have six of her original eight students returning that evening.

Creating jewelry had helped Connie through some difficult moments in her life, and she was delighted that, as a teacher, she had the opportunity pass on a craft that might aid others in doing the same. At the very least, it would be a blessing to have everyone together again. The group may only have gathered once, but they had been through a lot together.

Students were due to arrive at 7:00, and although it wasn't a scheduled shift for Grace, she insisted on attending to lend her moral support. Connie didn't object.

By 6:15, everything was set up and ready to go, which left Connie just enough time to heat up some leftovers for dinner and relax on her sofa before class.

In addition to the murder being solved, Connie was also on cloud nine, because her sister had texted her that morning to announce that the family would be spending Christmas in Sapphire Beach.

It seemed that the day couldn't get any better.

Connie had just finished her turkey tips and mashed potatoes when, through the front window, she saw Zach pull up in his gray Jeep and park in front of her store. He smiled broadly when he spotted Connie hanging out in the seating area.

Zach sat on an armchair facing Connie.

"You'll never guess where I just came from." Zach's easy smile told her that a weight had been lifted from his shoulders. She was pleased to see that he seemed like his old self again.

Before Connie could answer, he said, "I was just with Elyse looking at condos."

"In Sapphire Beach?" she asked, hopefully. "Does this mean you're staying?"

He nodded, another smile lighting up his face. "Yes, I decided to stay. After a lot of soul searching, I realized that, although I do miss my family, my life is here. I love my job, and I have some solid friends. Not to mention that I'm happier and healthier in this sunny climate."

Connie was elated at hearing the news. "You went from not knowing if you wanted to stay to committing to Sapphire Beach with a major purchase? Why such a dramatic change of heart?"

"Well, now that I know that Sapphire Beach is home, I don't see any reason not to fully commit. I decided to move out of my apartment and to purchase something larger. Not only will my family be able to visit without staying in a hotel, but I think it will help me to feel like I have roots here. The condo I toured today isn't right for me, but I'm excited to have gotten the process started."

Connie had never been to Zach's apartment, but he once referred to it as a shoebox. He rented it when he first took the job in Sapphire Beach, with the intention of saving up to eventually buy something bigger if he remained in the area.

"Has Elyse taken you to Palm Paradise?" she said, half joking.

Zach chuckled. "Palm Paradise is a little out of the price range of a police detective."

Connie laughed. "It's out of my price range, too. I'm just blessed to have had a generous aunt."

Zach stood to leave. "I'll let you get ready for your class. I just wanted to tell you my good news."

"So, I guess I'll be seeing you soon," she said as she walked him to the door.

He squeezed her forearm. "You can count on it." Then he added, "Thank you for your patience with me. I was really torn up about what to do, but I could have handled the whole thing better. I should have told you from the beginning what was going on."

Connie gave him an understanding smile. "I know what an agonizing decision it can be to relocate so far from family. Especially when nieces and nephews are in the picture."

"I'm going to take a couple of weeks' vacation next month to visit my family, but perhaps when I get back, we can have that second date."

"I'd like that," Connie said.

The crew from Florida Sands was coming down the sidewalk, so Zach gave Connie a warm smile and left.

Things were definitely turning around.

It was bittersweet seeing the group walk through the door without Allister and Isabel. Connie's only consolation was that justice had been served and Isabel was safely behind bars.

Judging from the solemn, yet relieved, expression that Abby, Paige and Mary Ann were wearing, Connie guessed that they felt the same. She hoped that tonight's class would, in some small way, contribute to their healing process.

Just behind the Florida Sands group was Jerry, followed by Gertrude, Elyse, Emma, and Victoria. Connie embraced her friends and greeted the rest of the group.

With great care, Mary Ann handed Connie a small bag. She opened it to discover the unfinished turquoise necklace that Allister had started two weeks before, on his last night on earth.

"He had dropped it off in his car after having dinner with Paige and before heading to the pier to meet Isabel," Mary Ann said solemnly. "We hoped you would finish it for him. We'd like to give it to his sister when she arrives tomorrow for his personal belongings."

Tears stung at the back of Connie's eyes. She carefully placed the necklace on the table in front of her chair. "What a beautiful gesture. It would be an honor."

She had chosen a relatively simple necklace design for her students, so Connie was optimistic that she could finish it that evening.

Grace brought out some cookies, along with some freshly brewed iced tea, while everyone diligently worked. Connie answered a few questions, then got to work on Allister's necklace.

When the iced tea pitchers were empty, Connie went out back to refill them, and Abby followed her.

"I could use a break," she said. "I'll give you a hand."

When they were out of ear shot of the others, Connie asked, "How are you doing after last night?"

"I'm okay. I'm still in shock that I was working with a killer the past few years, I guess. But I'm looking forward to putting this summer behind me and starting my senior year fresh. The President appointed one of my favorite professors as Interim Chair of the English Department, so I'm optimistic for next year. I may even consider doing my graduate studies at Florida Sands." Abby's gaze went down to the floor. "But I think I'll look for an off-campus job next semester."

"That's understandable. I'm so glad that you are looking forward to your senior year, though."

They filled the pitchers and started to head back to join the others, when Connie suddenly stopped. "I have a great idea! Come September, when the snowbirds start to return, I'll be looking for another part-time worker. I'd love it if you'd consider taking the job. It would be weekend and evening hours, perfect for a student."

Abby's eyes grew wide. "That sounds amazing. I would be a pro at jewelry making by the time I graduate," she said.

"Absolutely," Connie said as they headed back. "I'll teach you everything I know."

Connie smiled as she realized that she had only been a year older than Abby when she learned how to make jewelry from her friend, Dura, during her post-graduate term of volunteer service in Kenya. Dura was now one of *Just Jewelry's* top suppliers.

When they rejoined the others at the table, Emma excitedly declared, "I think I'm done." She showed her bracelet to Connie, out of view of the others. "I attached the jewelry findings like you taught me. Can you check and make sure I did everything right?"

Connie inspected the bracelet. "It's beautiful, honey."

"Emma has not let me see her bracelet since she was here on Sunday," Elyse said. "I wonder what she's up to." Elyse pretended she was trying to see the bracelet, but Emma playfully pulled it away.

Emma beamed as she proudly took her creation over to Victoria, who was sitting on Grace's lap, and fastened the bracelet around the child's tiny wrist. "It's fits perfectly!"

Victoria giggled at Emma's enthusiasm. Emma kissed her baby sister on the cheek and explained to

Elyse that she switched out the E bead for a V bead as a surprise for Victoria. "It's a gift to welcome my new baby sister to the family," Emma said.

"She loves it," Elyse said, tears welling in her eyes. She gave her eldest daughter a hug and a kiss on the top of her head. "I'm sure she'll treasure it always."

Everyone else managed to finish their creations, too. Gertrude was pleased with hers and decided to give it to a friend for her eightieth birthday, and Paige, Abby, and Mary Ann were delighted to have something new to spice up their wardrobes.

Jerry and Connie each also finished their projects before the end of the class. Connie wrapped the necklace that Allister began just two weeks before, not knowing it would be his last creative endeavor, and entrusted it to Mary Ann for safe keeping.

"When are you offering another class?" Abby asked Connie.

"With everything that happened this time around, I haven't had a chance to think about it."

"It would be a shame if you let what happened to Allister deter you," Mary Ann said. "There was

240

nothing you could have done to stop that from happening."

The others nodded in agreement.

"You're a fantastic teacher," Jerry said, holding up his finished project for everyone to admire. "Who would have thought I could make something this beautiful for my wife? You might have to vouch for me to prove that I made it myself. Liz is never going to believe it."

Jerry beamed with pride as the others praised his work.

"I would take another class in a heartbeat," Abby said. "And I'll tell my friends to join me."

"I'll tell you what," Connie said. "I'll plan another class for August and send you all the dates."

For the first time in two weeks, Connie was optimistic about her next class. She couldn't wait to see what the future held.

The End

Next Book in this Series

Book 4: *Candy Canes and Cadavers*
Available on Amazon

OR

Free Prequel: *Vacations and Victims*.
Meet Concetta and Bethany in the
Sapphire Beach prequel.
Available in ebook or PDF format only at:
BookHip.com/MWHDFP

Stay in touch!

Join my Readers' Group for periodic updates, exclusive content, and to be notified of new releases. Enter your email address at:
BookHip.com/MWHDFP

OR

Email:
angela@angelakryan.com

Facebook:
facebook.com/AngelaKRyanAuthor

Post Office:
Angela K. Ryan, John Paul Publishing, P.O. Box 283, Tewksbury, MA 01876

ABOUT THE AUTHOR

Angela K. Ryan, author of the *Sapphire Beach Cozy Mystery Series*, writes clean, feel-good stories that uplift and inspire, with mysteries that will keep you guessing.

When she is not writing, Angela enjoys the outdoors, especially kayaking, stand-up paddleboarding, snowshoeing, and skiing. She lives near Boston and loves the change of seasons in New England, but, like her main character, she looks forward to brief escapes to the white, sandy beaches of southwest Florida, where her mother resides.

Angela dreams of one day owning a Cavalier King Charles Spaniel like Ginger, but isn't home enough to take care of one. So, for now, she lives vicariously through her main character, Connie.

Made in the USA
Columbia, SC
24 November 2020